The Bottle Tree

By Robert D. Bennett

Publisher
Rebellion Books
www.RebellionBooks.com
Copyright 2011

ACKNOWLEDGMENTS

For Karren, Danielle, Robert, Anthony, Mom, Uncle Mike, Pa Willie, Ma Gracie, and Aunt Thelma as well as the others in my family who encouraged me to read and taught me to love history and the hills of Central Louisiana.

A special thanks to my first grade teacher, Mrs. McKillips, who recently passed away. She was a great inspiration to me.

PREFACE

I've often heard people say that Louisiana is a country unto itself, but that's not quite true. It's like a small continent, with the whole way of life varying between different parts. Shreveport is different from Natchitoches, which is different from the Kisatchie Hills. The world changes even more the further south you go until you hit New Orleans, which is like stepping back hundreds of years into our past.

The turpentine camp described in this story was real, and I had the great pleasure of knowing people who lived and worked there when they were much younger, most of them now gone. I have smelled the pine smell from the "peculiar shaped mass" sticking out into the creek, walked the hills, and ate huckleberries picked fresh from the bush.

Caleb, Johnny, and Leesie are loosely based on people I have known, and who will live forever in my memories.

CHAPTER 1

The Beginning and the End

Sometimes he came back and just wandered through the trees, smelling the scent of pine in the air, sweating in the Louisiana humidity and remembering back to a time when life was much simpler. Rather than the swamps and bayous most people picture as comprising his home state, to him this was Louisiana, the pine covered hills of the forest, a hawk circling overhead, the distant singing of birds, and the sound of wind through the treetops.

Now that his age was catching up to him it was a lot harder to climb the hills and creek banks. Although occasionally his arthritis kept the distance he traveled on his strolls to a minimum, this was rare. As soon as he opened the car door and stepped into the once familiar surroundings his aches and pains seemed to melt away, returning with a vengeance only after he reentered his vehicle to return home. He'd often wondered if the pangs would remain hidden if he stayed there.

The twilight of his life was upon him. His once sharp mind now wandered and his memory betrayed him at the most inopportune times. He knew that to the young lawyers in his firm he was a relic of a past age, someone to respectfully greet as they passed in the hallway, all the while confident within themselves that his day had passed and that he was only being kept around out of respect for past accomplishments, accomplishments made during a time when computers were something from science fiction, when a handshake served as well as a certified signature on a document,

1

and when his chosen profession was viewed with respect and some degree of awe rather than being the subject of jokes reserved for traveling salesmen.

He wanted to bring one of his favored grandchildren here and let them accompany their doddering old grandfather on his wanderings through the woods. The choice would have to be made with the utmost care, as the message he wanted to leave to his descendants and others was one of paramount importance to him.

One of the phrases he kept hearing from the young Turks at the office was "quality time". It appeared to be the way they reassured themselves the time they spent away from home at work, country clubs, golf courses, and social functions was justified if the little time they did spend with their families was "quality time", whatever that meant.

Up ahead he saw the shine of the water trickling down the gravelly bed of what was now called Camp Creek. He knew just around the bend the creek widened slightly and a peculiar shaped mass protruded into the water. At first it appeared to be a misshapen rock, but if one were to strike it with a sharp object even after all of these years the rich scent of turpentine would still waft out. This smell would remind his grandchildren of household cleaner, but brought to his mind the images of children at play, the warmth of his mother's hug, and the rough feel of his father's calloused hands as he would gently brush his cheek and look at him with love in his eyes.

He picked his way through the forest, stopping occasionally to rest. He hadn't bothered to remove his coat or tie, and was wearing the highly polished, black leather wing tip oxfords normally reserved for court appearances. He did take a moment to loosen his tie, then started up the narrow and overgrown pathway to the top of the hill. As he reached the crest he paused to catch his breath, looking at the ramshackle old building standing in the partially overgrown clearing before his eyes stopped to rest on a flash of red in a tree off to one side.

CHAPTER 2

They Meet Johnny

Caleb Gandy could hardly remember when his life wasn't constantly surrounded by the pungent scent of pine sap. Whether it came from the sawmill, off of the boards from which most of the camp's structures were made, or was the rich aroma of turpentine being manufactured, the sticky stuff perfumed his whole world, escape only possible when the smell of the creek or the forest took over. This, however, took a good walk since the smell drifted on the wind.

Turpentine camps were a unique method of employment in the early 1900s in the South, the camps springing up in the middle of the forests, the men working to harvest timber and make turpentine from the pine forests. The camps were almost a small town with the needs of all of the inhabitants being met by the company they worked for, at a price. The camps were there for a while, closing down when the timber ran out and the inhabitants moved on.

Caleb had made a visit to Kisatchie Creek as soon as school was out and now triumphantly made his way back through camp to his house with eight catfish, recently residents of the same creek, dragging behind him on a piece of string threaded through their mouths and out their gills.

"Hey Leesie," he yelled when he passed by one of the smaller houses, a huge black cauldron sending up steam as the woman stirred the pot full of men's clothes, the young girl standing next to her waving at him. Behind them were several clotheslines, the wash flapping gently in the breeze as it dried.

4

"Hi Mrs. Osborne, I'll bring you some fish over as soon as I clean them."

"Thank you Caleb, some fish will be nice," the woman answered.

"Leesie, why don't you go and see if you can help Caleb? Don't be a bother to his momma though."

"Yes'm," the girl said over her shoulder as she ran to catch up with him. They'd been friends since they were big enough to walk, but Leesie hadn't been able to fish today with Caleb because her momma had needed help with the laundry. It was the only way she had of making a living since Leesie's daddy had gotten killed in an accident at the sawmill two years ago.

In central Louisiana anything you couldn't put a steamboat in was called a creek and Kisatchie Creek, where Caleb had been fishing, would have been a river in many areas of the country. It was fed by a steady supply of water from springs and various smaller creeks, some no more than a trickle while others were knee-deep. It was to one of these middle sized creeks running along the edge the camp just behind his house Caleb and Leesie now made their way to clean his catch.

He'd done this a lot of times, as had Leesie, and had a set routine. Leesie veered from following Caleb to grab a wash pan from the back porch of Caleb's house.

"Howdy, Mrs. Gandy," she said as she ran onto the porch. Caleb's mom was sitting there in her rocker, shelling peas into a pan just like the one Leesie grabbed from the porch.

"Hello Eloise," his mother said, the fresh peas making a pinging sound as they popped from their shells and hit the bottom of the tin pan. "How was school today?"

"It was fine. If you'll excuse me, I need to go and help Caleb clean his fish."

"Did he catch enough for supper?"

"Looked like it. He said he was going to give

me and momma a couple, but he should have more than enough."

"Good, they'll taste good with some fried taters and greens. Tell him to mind and not cut himself this time, Eloise."

"Yes'm."

With this reply, Leesie was off and running again. Caleb's mom, the preacher, and their teacher, Mrs. McKillips, were the only ones who called her Eloise, to everyone else she was Leesie

By the time she got to the creek, Caleb was working on the last catfish, the others already cleaned and laid out on the leaves next to him on the bank. He took a break to suck the blood from a fresh cut on his thumb and Leesie decided to forego the warning from his mom.

"What did you catch them on?" she asked.

"Regular old earthworms," he said. "Must've been a school of them though because I caught all these in about 15 minutes, then didn't have another bite."

He swished his knife around in the creek water and carefully dried it on his pants leg before putting it back into his pocket. Most of the boys in the camp had Barlow knives, cheap pocketknives that wouldn't hold an edge, but Caleb's daddy had given him a real knife, one of his old ones, and he was more careful about keeping it clean and sharp than he was about not cutting himself with it. The myriad of scars across his fingers were a map of all of his successful fishing and hunting trips.

After rinsing the fish off he threw them into the pan, then grabbed the heads, entrails, and skins and threw them to the pack of dogs and cats which had been patiently waiting for him to complete his task. They knew from prior camp experience that if they waited they'd get the leftovers, but if they edged too close then a kick or whack with a stick was likely to be their only reward.

Caleb and Leesie made their way back up the

6

bank of the creek, picking their way through the dogs and cats squabbling over the remains of the fish and back to Caleb's house.

"Momma, the fish are in the kitchen," he shouted as he entered the house, his mother no longer on the porch and not in sight.

He heard his daddy's voice yell from the front porch, "Caleb, come here for a minute."

The home they lived in was little more than a shack by city standards, but here in the turpentine camp it was one of the largest, with a living room, a kitchen with a table, and two bedrooms. Still, it only took a few seconds for Caleb and Leesie to walk from the kitchen to the front porch. As Caleb pushed open the screen door he saw his momma and daddy standing at the edge of the porch talking with a black man. At his feet was a box of fresh picked greens, and peeking from behind his legs was a boy about Caleb's age, as black as soot.

"Caleb, Leesie, this is Luther Robinson and his son Johnny. Luther's about to start working with us at the camp. His wife Dora grows the best greens and vegetables anywhere around. Johnny is gonna drop some by here every now and then with some vegetables for us and you help him get them in the house, all right?"

"Yes'sir," both Caleb and Leesie said.

"Your mom will get these," Mr. Gandy said as Caleb reached for the greens, "but it'd be a favor if you'd take Johnny and show him where everything is while I do the same for Luther."

Caleb and Leesie jumped off the porch and started down the trail to the camp, but stopped after a few steps when they realized Johnny hadn't moved from his position behind his daddy's legs.

"Sorry suh," Luther Robinson said. "He's not much used to new folks, and he's a little shy." While he said this he was patiently peeling his son's arms from around his leg.

Leesie stepped forward and grabbed Johnny's hand.

"Come on," she said, giving a tug on his right hand. He followed quietly.

"How old are you?" Caleb asked as they walked.

Johnnie shrugged his shoulders.

"Do you know how old you are?" Caleb asked.

Another shrug.

"Can you talk?"

A slight nod of the head.

"Then why don't you?"

Another shrug.

Caleb stopped, causing Leesie to stop dragging Johnny behind her.

"This isn't going to work," Caleb said in frustration.

"Hush Caleb," Leesie said quietly, then moved to stand directly in front of Johnny.

"Are you scared?" she asked.

Johnny nodded.

"Is it because we're strangers?"

A shrug.

"Is it because we're white strangers?"

A nod.

"Have you ever played with any white kids?"

A negative shake of the head.

"How about this? We'll pretend you're white and you pretend we're black. That way we can talk, okay?"

He started to nod his head but Leesie caught his face between her hands and said, "You have to say okay."

"Okay," he mumbled from between smushed cheeks. Leesie removed her hands from his face.

"That's a start. Now we'll tell you our names and you tell us yours. I'm Leesie."

"My name's Caleb."

8

"I'm Johnny".

"I knew you could talk," Leesie said in a tone that let on she was pleased with herself.

"You really don't know how old you are?" Caleb asked.

"I forget sometimes. I think I'm 10 though."

"That sounds about right," Caleb said. "I'm 11, and you're little shorter than me."

"Where are you from?" Leesie asked.

"Up the road a ways. Not really from nowhere."

"Did y'all move here to work in the camp?" Caleb asked. "My daddy is a foreman here. That's like a boss."

"My grand-mammy got sick, so we moved to her place to help out. It's over that way." He pointed back to the east.

"Your grandma's Mrs. Gaskey?" Caleb asked, naming the only black family that lived in that direction, about a half-mile from camp.

Johnny nodded.

"That's her. My momma's momma."

"I know Mrs. Gaskey, she makes the best fried apple pies around. She showed Momma how to make them one time when we went there to buy some vegetables and look for arrowheads when the garden got plowed."

"She used to, but she's sick now. Momma and Daddy are going to tend to the garden, but yo' daddy said we could move into town over there once't she got better."

He pointed toward a part of the camp setback from the rest. It was called Vinegar Hill although the origin of the name was a mystery since it wasn't on a hill and there wasn't any vinegar around. It was the part of the camp where the black families lived. The houses were smaller, the land muddier and there were more mosquitoes than in the section where Leesie and Caleb lived, but the situation was what it was and

9

nobody thought it odd in that day and time

While they walked, Caleb acted as a town guide, pointing out the various houses and structures and offering advice as to the quirks of the inhabitants.

"That's Miss Pryor's house, watch out for her dog, he bites." As if to illustrate his point a big yellow dog suddenly sprang from under the porch, and was stopped from attacking them only by the piece of rope tied around his neck and on the other end to a big log in the yard.

"Her dog's mean, but she's real nice. If you need her just stand out here and holler and she'll come out."

A little farther along.

"That's the Finstrom's house. They're real quiet, but nice. She don't like nothing on her front porch but her rocker and her cats, so if you leave vegetables for her, leave them around back."

Sure enough, the front porch was spotless except for one rocker sitting by itself, and a half-dozen cats laying around.

"She dips snuff too, so mind you don't get splashed if you're talking to her when she spits." Leesie motioned to a darkened patch of dirt in the front yard, the root sticking up from the ground the obvious target of Mrs. Finstrom's expectorations

The next shack in the town was not maintained as well as the others, the yard overgrown in places and piles of bottles over to one side. Even the outhouse in the side yard showed evidence of disrepair, the door barely hanging on and the building tilting to the left as if the next blue norther would blow it over.

"That's Mr. Latham's house. He used to be married but his wife ran off with a man that passed through here last year and promised he wouldn't beat on her like Mr. Latham did. He's mean even when he's not drunk and he's *always* drunk when he's not at work and sometimes when he is."

Caleb realized he had said something wrong

10

and looked at Leesie, who had a pained expression on her face.

"Sorry," he said.

"It's all right," she replied, although it was obvious she was suddenly close to tears. "Go ahead and tell him."

"You sure?"

She nodded.

Caleb turned back to Johnny.

"Mr. Latham and Leesie's daddy were working at the sawmill together a couple of years ago when the saw blade hit a knot and kicked the wood back out. It hit her daddy and killed him. Some people said that Mr. Latham had been drinking at work and had forgotten to put the guard back into place."

"I'm sorry," Johnny said to Leesie.

"Anyways, he's mean, mean, mean, so don't ever come here by yourself. He doesn't like anyone and he's especially mean to colored folks. If you've ever got anything to bring here, and you probably won't, let me know and I'll bring it for you."

"Okay," Johnny said, relief evident on his face. The more he could avoid conflict with white folks the better off he and his family would be.

They continued through the camp in a circular fashion, skipping Vinegar Hill since Caleb never went there, and ended up at the schoolhouse.

"And this is Leesie's favorite place, the schoolhouse," Caleb said.

"I'm going to be a schoolteacher when I grow up," Leesie said.

"She's the smartest one in our school," Caleb added, proudly.

"Are you going to school with us?" Leesie asked.

"Leesie, you know the colored kids aren't allowed at our school," Caleb said.

"Where do they go to school?" Leesie asked.

Johnny looked embarrassed and shook his

head.

"We don't," Johnny said in a whisper.

"You've never been to school?" Leesie asked.

"Uh uh," Johnny shook his head.

"Do you know how to read?"

"Uh uh."

"Do you want to learn?"

Johnny looked at her suspiciously.

"What fo'?"

"So you can be smart."

"My Daddy's smart and he can't read."

"But he'd be smarter if he could."

"What would I read?"

"Most anything with writing on it," Leesie said, getting excited. "You can read about history, that's what happened in the past, you can read stories about other places, you can read the Bible. There's lots to read."

"I'd sho' like to be able to read the Bible to see if it say what the preacher say it do."

"Then I'll teach you how to read," Leesie said. "It'll be fun. Then I'll teach you how to write and how to do arithmetic. You'll be a learning fool before you know it."

Leesie was satisfied, it showed on her face, and Johnny beamed at the idea, his white teeth shining in bright contrast to his dark face. Caleb wasn't sure why Johnny was so happy, school was just a bother to him, interfering with all the other stuff he'd rather be doing with his time.

A few more minutes and they passed the church the white folks used, not the black church which was smaller and really more of an open air brush arbor located at the far end of Vinegar Hill. Caleb knew from the singing that poured forth every Sunday that the colored church services lasted all day, whereas his church was over by lunch. He enjoyed Sunday school just fine since the time was spent fraternizing and hearing stories like David and Goliath, but the church itself was stuffy, he had to sit still and be quiet, and he never really understood what the preacher was talking about.

Even worse was when it was their turn for the preacher to visit for Sunday lunch. His mom was famous for her fried chicken and chicken and dumplings and the preacher made sure his hand was sneaking for the biggest piece of chicken on the plate during the prayer, ready to clamp down and claim his prize as soon as the "amen" was muttered. Plus, he ate as much as two men, ensuring no leftovers for later that day.

Just past the church was a camp store stocked with the basics and a few frivolities. If the residents of the camp needed anything not available they'd ask Mr. Jenkins, who ran the store, to order it from Natchitoches, two days away on horseback, and have it delivered. He kept a catalog behind the counter that Caleb would often leaf through, imagining a world where all those things were actually available and the types of people who could afford them. Of course, there was also the Sears and Roebuck catalog, which provided entertainment as much as anything else, but an order from them took several weeks to arrive and so was only used for exceptional purchases.

Caleb motioned Johnny to follow him and Leesie up the steps, across a wide painted porch and through the double screen doors into the dark, cool confines of the store. He let the door close behind him, careful that it didn't slam.

There was a grown man at the counter, his back to the children, in a discussion with Mr. Jenkins. From the tone of the voices Caleb could tell the conversation was less than friendly.

"No, Ed. Not until you make some kind of payment."

"Have a heart Jenkins. I'm not asking for much."

"Your bill is already the highest one I've got,

13

and you live by yourself. You have to make some kind of payment at least once a month, you know the rules."

"But I'm flat busted right now."

"Sorry Ed. If you weren't giving old Ukiah and Callie Monroe all your money..."

The man's tone turned even meaner as he growled, "What I do with my money is my own damn business."

As he spoke his left hand clenched into a fist and slammed on the counter, causing the glass jars of candy to rattle, while his right dropped to the hilt of a large knife strapped to his hip in a scabbard.

Mr. Jenkins took a step back, then the sound of the screen door slamming at the entrance of the store caused both him and Ed Latham to look around.

"Howdy Mr. Jenkins...Ed," said Caleb's daddy, slowly pulling a plug of chewing tobacco from his pocket and cutting a piece with his own knife, popping it into his mouth before offering the plug to Ed Latham, who turned it down with a shake of his head and a grunt.

"Thought I'd bring Luther here by and let you know he was working for us now," Mr. Gandy said as he walked to the counter running diagonal to the one where Mr. Jenkins and Latham had been arguing. "So he'll need an account set up, and likely some supplies to start out."

"Sure thing Mr. Gandy. I'll get him set up with whatever he needs."

"You might want to talk to him about his vegetables too. His wife Dora has taken over for Mrs. Gaskey. They'd probably be amenable to planting whatever it is you have the hardest time getting. At a fair price of course."

"Of course, of course. I'll do just that. Luther, you pick out whatever you need and if you can't find it I'll order it from Natchitoches and it should be here within the week. We settle up accounts after the first payday of each month."

14

"Yas'suh," Luther Robinson replied and began walking through the store selecting an item here and there, occasionally picking one up and putting it back after some thought. Johnny stayed planted with Caleb and Leesie, although he watched his dad for any sign he needed help.

"I'll meet you outside Luther," Caleb's daddy said, then dug around in the pocket of his denim overalls and fished a nickel out, tossing it on the counter. "Mr. Jenkins, give these kids some candy, make sure you start stocking Johnny's favorite too."

He turned and left the store.

"Will do, Mr. Gandy," Mr. Jenkins called after him.

Caleb was watching Ed Latham, and held his arm out to stop Leesie from pulling Johnny up to the glass candy jars.

Latham was looking back and forth between Luther Robinson and Mr. Jenkins. Luther appear to be studying the label of a can, but since Johnny had told them he couldn't read the kids knew he was likely killing time, hoping Ed Latham would leave.

"Isn't this a fine goddamn situation? Good, hard-working white folks can't get no credit here but every nigger that walks in is treated like a goddamn king."

Mr. Jenkins didn't reply and Luther Robinson just kept looking at the can, as if in too deep a thought to even hear Latham's words.

"Is that right nigger? Is you a king?" He put his hand back on the hilt of his knife and took a step to Mr. Robinson's direction.

"I reckon that's about enough," said Caleb's daddy from behind them, where he'd slipped quietly back in the store.

Latham stopped moving.

"Don't you have somewhere to be, Ed?"

He didn't reply just turned to leave the store, careful not to brush against Mr. Gandy as he passed.

15

"And Ed?"

Latham stopped, but didn't turn to face Mr. Gandy.

"What?"

"I'd appreciate if you didn't cuss or call anyone a nigger in camp."

Ed's shoulders hunched up as if a spasm had struck him.

"What I do on my off hours is my own damn business."

"True enough, except when you do it on company property. And last time I checked the company owned this whole damned camp. So, again, I'd appreciate it if you didn't cuss or call anyone a nigger in this camp."

Ed Latham didn't reply.

"Did you hear me, Ed?" The voice had a touch more steel in it than before. Caleb had heard that tone enough to know his father was at the edge of his patience.

"I heard you."

"Good enough then." This time the tone indicated the conversation was over and Ed Latham was dismissed.

He stomped out of the store, slamming the screen door behind him.

As Mr. Gandy walked to the counter, he nodded at Luther, who put the can down then continued piling stuff on one arm. He nodded back at Mr. Gandy in thanks.

"Glad I came back in," Caleb's daddy said and flipped another coin on the counter. "Give these kids a soda pop on me too."

16

CHAPTER 3

A First for Johnny

The three kids sat on a downed log, a bag of candy grasped in one hand, a bottle of soda pop in the other.

"So what do you think?" Caleb asked Johnny. He'd been astonished to discover Johnny had never even seen a soda pop before, much less drank one. He'd used his vast knowledge to recommend a grape soda for Johnny's first.

"It's the best thing I ever had," Johnny replied.

They'd also been surprised to find that Johnny had only had one piece of candy before, a peppermint stick for his birthday a few years ago.

"Well, to be a good customer you have to know what to choose from," Mr. Jenkins had said. He'd gotten three small paper bags and put several pieces of each kind of hard candy he'd had in stock in each of the bags. Caleb knew it was lots more candy than the nickel's worth his daddy had paid for. Each time the storekeeper had dropped another piece of candy into the bags, Johnny's eyes had gotten a little wider.

"You be sure to remember which ones you liked and which ones you didn't so you'll know next time you order."

They thanked him and were headed out the door when Mr. Jenkins called Caleb back. Leesie and Johnny continued on outside, the boy now following her without the requirement that she drag him by the hand.

"Caleb, I expect you ought to warn your little friend about Ed Latham."

"I did," Caleb assured the man.

"As a matter of fact, there are several people in camp not far from Ed in their way of thinking. Tell him that if he comes in to look for me and if I shake my head he's to go wait outside and I'll get to him directly."

Caleb had explained it to Johnny while they were looking for a good place to sit down. Johnny took the news in stride, acting surprised only that he was to be allowed in the store by himself at all.

Some of the other kids had gathered together to shoot marbles in the waning light. Night came faster in the camp because of the thick cover the pine trees provided.

The three children approached the other group, not thinking about the fact that all of them were white.

"Who's winning?" Caleb asked Riley Wells, one of his friends.

"Ben Johnson, again," he replied.

"He's using a ball bearing that he claims is a steel marble and the other kids are afraid to say anything to him."

Sure enough, Caleb watched as the shiny steel ball knocked another aggie from the circle drawn in the dirt, which the bigger boy promptly grabbed up, glee apparent, and put into a leather bag swinging from his belt.

Ben knew better than to try using that trick on the older boys, but the younger ones were only now learning not to play with him if they wanted to keep their marble collections safe.

The loser of the game, his sack of marbles depleted, and not likely to be replenished soon due to the cost, ran off trying not to cry. Ben Johnson got to his feet holding his hands over his head in triumph.

Caleb blew air between his lips in what would be known in town as a "raspberry" and drew Ben's attention.

"Say Caleb, want to share that soda?"

"Not particularly," Caleb replied, turning the

18

bottle up and driving the last quarter. "And before you ask, Leesie doesn't want to either." She shook her head in agreement.

"I sure ain't gonna ask the nigger," Ben said, looking over his shoulder at the other children to be sure they were watching.

"Don't say nigger," Leesie scolded. "It's not a nice word."

Ben looked at Johnny, sneered and said, "Nigger, nigger, nigger!"

Caleb handed what was left of his bag of candy to Leesie and stepped between Johnny and Ben.

"Ben, my daddy asked me to look after Johnny, so I 'spect that he'd say when you're mean to him it's the same as if you're doing it to me. Do you want me to have to make you eat dirt until you cry again?" Caleb reminded the slightly bigger boy of their last fight which had been provoked by him snatching one of Leesie's dolls from her.

Ben looked decidedly uncomfortable at the idea of fighting Caleb again.

"This ain't your fight," he said to Caleb.

"I think it is. I think that any time I catch you picking on Johnny or Leesie it will be my fight."

"What are you, some kind of nigger lover?"

"My mom says only stupid people use that word. I guess she's right. Johnny is my friend, now do you want to get after it or go on home for supper?"

"You wouldn't be such hot stuff if your Pa wasn't the boss."

"I didn't notice him having much to do with me whipping you before."

Just then Caleb heard his mom's voice off in the distance, calling him home for supper.

"I've got to go. Do you want me to whip you first or not?"

One of the younger boys gathered behind Ben suddenly pushed him toward Caleb, but the larger boy swerved in the direction of his house instead.

19

"I ain't afraid of you," he said over his shoulder as he stomped off. "But if I'm late for supper, my Pa will tan me."

The group of kids broke up, each making their way home for the night. Caleb, Johnny and Leesie headed to his house, where Luther Robinson and Mr. Gandy stood in the front yard talking, one of Luther's hands holding the reins to a skinny, sickly looking mule. As they came up Luther reached down and swung Johnny up and onto the mule, the remnants of the candy sack still clutched tightly in his hand.

While Caleb went and stood by his father, Leesie disappeared into the house, returning a few moments later with a plate on which two fried fish were situated.

"Your momma fried our fish for us," Leesie said. "I better get them home so we can eat. Bye!"

She leapt from the porch and ran off into the darkness, her blonde hair flowing behind her. Johnny waved at her from the mule, one cheek swollen out from the jawbreaker he'd stuffed in there.

"I sure do 'preciate what you and Mrs. Abigail has done for me and mine. And what Missuh Caleb doin' for Johnny," Luther said as he finished tightening up the load on the mule's back behind Johnny.

"It may not be easy on you Luther, but you'll get an honest day's pay for an honest day's work. Still, you can expect some of the white folks to resent you getting the job while some of them do the harder work. You particularly look out for Ed Latham. He's not going to be happy about being demoted again and even less happy that you're getting his job."

"I'll be careful."

Luther touched the brim of his hat and dipped his head again to Caleb's dad then to Caleb before taking the bridle of the mule to begin the long walk back to Mrs. Gaskey's house. As they disappeared into the rapidly darkening distance Johnny could be heard describing the candy and soda pop to his dad, who

20

chuckled occasionally at his son's excitement.

"Ready to eat?" Caleb's daddy asked him, laying a big, rough hand on his shoulder.

"Starving."

The catfish had been coated in cornmeal and pan fried until crispy on the outside, white and delicious on the inside. Abigail Gandy had also sliced some potatoes thin and pan fried them with onions, cooked a mess of greens, and served a huge piece of corn bread drowning in butter on the side, topping it all off with glasses of milk, kept cold by hanging the pitcher down the well at the end of a rope.

"So what job is Luther going to do?" Abigail asked her husband during supper.

"He's going to be leading a mule team hauling logs."

"You starting a new team?"

"Naw, Ed Latham showed up drunk again the other day and forgot to latch the chain. Some logs got away and like to have killed the crew coming up the hill behind him. The logs did break a leg on one of the mules and we had to shoot it. So Ed is going on ax duty, cutting the limbs off of downed trees. That way the only person he can hurt is hisself."

"Why don't you just fire him?"

"We're shorthanded as it is. If we get a new bunch of people Ed will be the first one I let go."

"Has there ever been a black man leading a mule team?"

"No, but it's time and Luther Robinson's a good hand with the mules and a hard worker to boot."

"An all colored crew?"

"Of course. Can't take things too fast. There really would be hell to pay if I put a black man in a position to boss white men."

Caleb had been plowing through his food, but was finishing up, crumbling the last of his cornbread in the pot liquor from the greens.

"Why do some people call colored folks

21

niggers?" He asked his parents around a mouthful of cornbread.

"Some people don't know any better and some just don't care. Others just do it because they're mean or uneducated," his daddy replied.

"And some do it because they want to use a hateful word to make themselves feel like there are people lower than them," his mother added.

"I don't want to hear you saying it though," Mr. Gandy added quickly.

"No sir, I wouldn't. Momma's right, it's an ugly word that doesn't really fit the colored folks I know."

"Son, what did you think of Johnny?"

"He's nice. Kind of quiet, but nice. Did you know he'd never had a soda pop before?"

"I didn't know, but it doesn't surprise me. Do you think y'all are going to be friends?"

"I think we already are."

"That's good. Just be prepared for people not to like it. If any adults give you trouble you let me know, but the kids may be hard on you for being friends with him. It may be rough on you and I won't blame you if you don't spend too much time with him."

"I can handle the kids. They used to give me a lot of lip about Leesie being my friend and us playing together, but they hardly even notice now."

"This may be worse than that. With Leesie they were just teasing you and probably didn't have anything against Leesie herself."

"But they don't even know Johnny, why would they have anything against him?"

His dad stood up from the table and walked to the counter, helping himself to another fried fish.

"The people that will give you trouble about Johnny don't have to know him not to like him, the same as some people won't like Luther, Dora, or any of the others on Vinegar Hill. Just their skin color will be enough to get 'em riled. It's gonna be even worse for

Johnny because a lot of the white folks are going to be mad Luther has a white man's job. You just be careful and watch yourselves."

"We will."

CHAPTER 4

Ukiah's Cabin

They didn't see Johnny again for a couple of weeks but then, one Saturday, Caleb walked out of the house to see Johnny sitting in the dirt outside his gate.

"Hey Johnny," Caleb said.

"Hey."

"What you doing sitting outside there?"

"Waitin' on you."

"Why didn't you let me know you were here?"

"Daddy always said it's not a good idea to bother white folks."

"Dang it Johnny, if we're going to be friends you've got to stop all this black folks and white folks talk, leastways while you're with me and Leesie."

"I'll try, but it's sho' gonna be hard."

"You just keep trying and I'll just keep reminding you. Okay?"

Johnny nodded.

"Let's go get Leesie."

Leesie was sitting on her front porch playing school house with her doll.

"Don't you get enough of that during the week?" Caleb asked.

"Uh uh. I wish we had school everyday. Hey Johnny."

"Hey," Johnny replied.

"You want me to start schooling you today, Johnny?" She asked.

"No, no, no," Caleb jumped in before Johnny could answer. "There's something just not right about having school on Saturday. Y'all can start next week."

Caleb didn't notice the look of disappointment that passed over Johnny's face. What was a chore to someone required to do it could be a treat to someone to whom it was forbidden. This was a lesson learned as you grew older, and the innocent age of the three friends meant it wasn't likely to be understood, even if someone had put it into words.

"Y'all want to go to Ukiah's with me?" Caleb asked.

"Sure," Leesie replied.

"Who's that?" Johnny asked.

"He lives outside of camp just a little ways. He's older than anybody else around, but he's fun."

"Sure is. You'll like him." Leesie added.

"You sho' it'll be okay if'n I come?"

"Sure will," Caleb said, no doubt in his voice.

The three made their way through camp, Johnny looking with longing at the store as they passed and licking his lips, unnoticed by either Caleb or Leesie. They didn't know he'd kept the soda pop bottle, insisting on filling it with water and drinking out of it at home.

They wound their way through the woods, dodging sawbriar patches and snaky looking places, slowly making their way uphill. Eventually they stepped out into a pasture with a log cabin perched close to the edge of the hill. In the distance was a field, and up next to the house was a mule, methodically walking in a circle while a gray-haired man fed some type of stalks into a grinder. As the kids approached, Johnny could see a bucket under the contraption, brown liquid pouring from the grinder into the bucket. A shotgun leaned up against the fence.

"What's he doin'?" Johnny asked

"Making syrup. Come on, this is always fun."

The kids ran across the field, Johnny lagging behind, not entirely sure about running up to a white stranger with a shotgun close at hand.

"Howdy Ukiah," Caleb yelled as he ran up.

25

"Hi Ukiah," Leesie said.

"Well, well, well, look what we have here. Children all over the place," the man said as he grabbed the bridle of the mule, bring it to a stop.

"Now I know you and you," he pointed at Caleb and Leesie, "but I don't know you a'tall."

Johnny shrank back.

"He's scared of white folks," Leesie said matter-of-factly.

"He is?" Ukiah asked.

Johnny didn't say anything, just huddled against the fence, hiding behind a rail post.

Ukiah squatted down and look through the fence.

"Know something?" he asked Johnny in a quiet voice, eyes level with the boy's.

Johnny shook his head.

"I'm scared of white folks too," he smiled as he said this, and stood up to his full height.

Johnny did too.

"You is?" the boy asked.

"Sure. I'm half Comanche Indian, half Mexican, and half Barbary pirate. I'm pretty sure there has to be a little colored thrown in there somewhere. Now come over here, let's be friends."

Johnny climbed through the fence and went to where Caleb and Leesie were busy using his pocketknife to whittle off pieces of the sugarcane from a pile to one side of the mill. Caleb peeled a couple of pieces and handed them to Leesie and Johnny to chew on before trimming a piece for himself.

"You kids want to help? There's a jar of cane syrup in it for each of you if you do." Ukiah asked

"Sure," Caleb said, as Leesie and Johnny nodded in agreement.

They spent the rest of the morning pushing sugar cane into the mill, ducking each time the boom attached to the mule passed overhead, occasionally taking the bucket with the cane juice to a huge black cauldron and dumping it in. Caleb and Leesie knew from experience that Ukiah would put a fire under the cauldron later and cook the liquid down until only sweet, thick syrup was left.

When the sun was directly overhead, they broke for lunch, Ukiah slicing pieces off of a huge ham he took from the smoke house and putting them between slices of bread slathered with fresh butter. After they had finished eating they retired to the shade of the porch and sat around while Ukiah told stories of his adventures, sometimes as a soldier, sometimes as a pirate. None of them knew, or really cared, whether the stories were true but it wouldn't have mattered anyway because the stories were fascinating.

Every now and then the tall tales would be interrupted when one of the men from the camp would wander up. When he noticed them, Ukiah would stop his storytelling, politely excuse himself and walk with the man to a wooden shed not far from the house.

"What's he doin'?" Johnny asked when a third man had interrupted the stories.

"Come see," Caleb said, and the three kids jumped off the porch and went back to where they could see into the shed.

Inside the building were shelves, and on the shelves were jars, some with clear liquid, others with liquid the color of the syrup they'd been working on. Caleb pointed toward a big metal contraption sitting in the open not far from the building. It was copper colored and had several parts, one of which was a large coil of copper tubing. The burned wood and ashes under it made it clear that fires were built to heat the content of the pot.

"It's moonshine whiskey," Leesie whispered. "And some other kind called 'Rum' that Ukiah makes from the sugar cane. He says he learned how when he was a pirate in the Car-ra-bean, wherever that is."

"Oh," Johnny said. He had heard of moonshine but had never seen it.

27

A few minutes later the man had selected a jar of the clear liquid, handed Ukiah some coins, and made his way back down the hill.

"I know, I know," Ukiah said as he made his way back to the kids. "The preacher says likker is a sin, but they're always drinking wine in the Bible so I 'spect it's not the drinking that's the sin but the drunkenness. Besides, the preacher knows what I do for a living and he's never returned any of the money I put in that plate he's always passing around." Ukiah walked back to the front porch, the kids following behind.

"Anything else happening?" Caleb asked, trying to act nonchalant but failing miserably.

Leesie looked at Johnny and winked.

"No, not much," Ukiah replied, rocking and looking into the distance. "I 'spect it's gonna be a hot summer though."

"That's what daddy says," Caleb replied. Disappointment was clear in his voice.

"Well, let me get some syrup for you. Your mommas should be pleased, they know old Ukiah makes the best syrup around."

He disappeared into the house, reappearing a moment later with three jars of the rich, brown liquid.

"Here y' are," he said, handing a bottle to Caleb and Leesie. Before he handed the third jar to Johnny he paused.

"You're not afraid of my syrup are you?"

"Naw suh," Johnny replied.

"Not afraid of me no more?"

"Naw suh."

"You gonna come back and visit me?"

"Yas'suh."

"Are you Luther and Dora's boy?"

"Yas'suh."

"Be sure and let your parents know I'm in the market for fresh vegetables too. Be glad to pay cash or swap, whichever they'd rather. If your grandmomma makes any fried pies I'd sure appreciate a few. I can cook good for an old bachelor, but I never could get the hang of fried pies."

Ukiah handed him the jar and patted him on the head, the first time a white man had ever touched him in a friendly way. He went back into the house, returning a minute later with a pan.

"Y'all try this, it's a candy I learned to make from an old voodoo woman in Mississippi. It's just boiled syrup with some roasted peanuts ground up in it, but it's tasty."

The pan was passed around and everybody agreed it was fine candy. Sticky, but fine nonetheless.

After they had finished the candy the stories started up again along with lessons on how to fish, the best places to put beaver traps, and a host of other subjects.

Eventually Ukiah seemed to tire of talking and the warm afternoon began to take its toll as they all started getting drowsy.

Caleb was just about to announce it was time to leave when Ukiah stood and snapped his fingers as if he'd suddenly remembered something important.

"You kids in a hurry?"

They assured him they were not.

"Come help me with a little chore."

CHAPTER 5

The Bottle Tree

"What is it?" Leesie asked, walking around the tree and examining it from all angles. Caleb and Johnny did the same.

Ukiah had decorated a tree with bottles. Some were tied on with string, some were stuck on the end of cut off branches. The bottles were a mixture of sizes, shapes, and colors. Some blue, some clear, some brown. On one side of the small tree sitting on the ground was a solitary, bright red one.

"Y'all ain't never seen one of these?"

"I have," Johnny volunteered, surprising both Caleb and Leesie.

"You have? Where at?" Ukiah asked.

"My Uncle Franklin used to have one in his yard. Not as big or pretty as yours though. He called it his 'bottle tree'".

"And that's exactly what it is. Did he tell you what it was for?"

"He said it kept the spirits away."

"It does that, plus more. You see these bottles here?" Ukiah pointed to the clear, blue, and brown ones on the tree. "The bad spirits hear the wind whistling through these and it scares them off. If'n they do come around, the wind pushes them into the bottles and they're trapped there and can't bother you."

"What about that one? It's pretty," Leesie pointed to the red one on the ground.

"Oooo, you got a good eye, Leesie. That's the one that makes *my* bottle tree special. Most of them are just to take care of bad spirits but that red one is the cat's meow. It's for good spirits."

"Good spirits?" Johnny asked. "I ain't never heerd of no good spirits."

"That old voodoo woman who taught me how to make that peanut candy told me a real bottle tree has to have a special red bottle. According to her, and I 'spect she's right, sometimes people die and their bodies can't be given a proper church burial so they can't go straight to heaven. Their spirit wanders around until it finds the red bottle and it stays inside it until somebody they love dies and their spirit comes looking for them and helps them get to heaven. Don't that sound nice?"

"Yes sir. It'd sure be lonely just to wander around by your lonesome," Caleb said.

"It sure would. That's why everyone ought to know where there's a bottle tree like mine. Just in case."

Caleb's head suddenly whipped around in the direction of the barn, as if he'd heard something. He took a few steps in that direction, then stopped and continued to listen to Ukiah, occasionally glancing at the ramshackle barn located not far from them.

"We need to put the bottle somewhere so's the good spirits can see it from a ways off. Where do you think it should go?"

Both Johnny and Leesie looked at Caleb for direction, but his attention was still focused on the barn.

"Caleb, where do you think it should go?" Leesie asked.

"Huh? Oh. Why don't you pick a place? Or Johnny?"

"That's a good idea. Johnny, where do you think it should go?"

Johnny made two complete circles around the tree, proud that he'd been asked to help with such an important task and serious about doing his best. He finally pointed at a place on the side nearest the house, midways on the tree.

"Looks good to me," Ukiah said. He slipped a

31

leather thong from his pocket and tied it around the neck of the bottle.

"Why don't you do the honors?" He handed the bottle to Leesie, then lifted her up to where she could tie the leather thong in the place Johnny had indicated.

"Caleb, are you going to help?" Leesie asked as she was being lowered back to the ground.

"Caleb's got his mind on other things," Ukiah said. "I meant for it to be a surprise, but go ahead boy. She's in there with her new family."

Caleb's face split into a wide grin and he bolted for the barn as Leesie, Ukiah, and Johnny stepped back to admire their handiwork and the way the red bottle glistened in the sun.

"It sure looks pretty hanging there, doesn't it?" Ukiah asked, and both Leesie and Johnny agreed with him.

"Now the good spirits will know where to come," Leesie said with finality.

"Mayhaps they will child, mayhaps they will, That's the story anyway."

"Where'd Caleb go?" Johnny asked, looking around.

"Down to the barn," Ukiah said and pointed. "Why don't you two go see what he's doing?"

The two took off and raced to the barn, where they found Caleb kneeling in the dirt looking at a momma dog surrounded by a wiggling mass of newborn puppies.

"Ukiah said one of them is mine," he proudly told Johnny.

"Which one?" Johnny asked.

"I'm not sure yet."

"That's good Caleb," Ukiah said as he walked up. "Wait until they get older and show their personality, don't just pick one because you like the way they look. Appearances don't count for much, it's what's inside that counts."

"They're blue tick hounds," Caleb said

authoritatively. "The best 'coon hounds in the world, right Ukiah?"

"To my mind they are, but they'll hunt anything. A blue tick is one of the most gentle dogs there is, but they're mean if the situation calls for it. I saw a man hit one with stick and get his arm laid open clear to the bone. Twenty minutes later the same dog was laying down letting little kids crawl all over him and drag him around by the ears."

"These are pure bred and worth fifty dollars," Caleb said.

"Fifty dollars?" Johnny echoed. "For a dog? Ain't nobody got enough money to spend fifty dollars on a dog, no matter who they is."

"You'd be surprised," Ukiah said. "Some of those rich folks spend a lot more than that on dogs that ain't half as good or useful as blue ticks. Some folks got more money than sense, but all of these dogs are already promised for fifty dollars each, as soon as they are weaned off of their momma."

"Except mine," Caleb said.

"Except yours," Ukiah agreed. "They should be weaned in six or seven weeks and you can take your pick home then."

"I know I want a boy and I'm gonna name him Bo and we're going hunting as soon as he's old enough."

"Can I come?" Johnny asked.

"Sure you can, we'll have a good time."

"What about me?" Leesie asked.

"Well, we go 'coon hunting at night, and you know your momma don't let you out at night, but you can come squirrel hunting with me during the day."

Leesie nodded that that would be fine with her.

They lightly petted the puppies, occasionally holding one for a few seconds as their momma, Queenie, looked carefully on then inspected and licked the puppies clean after they set them back down.

Eventually, Ukiah mentioned that it was getting

on up in the afternoon and they might want to start back home so their mommas wouldn't be worried.

Reluctantly they put the puppies down, washing up only after Ukiah insisted and furnished them with a bucket of water and a bar of strong lye soap.

"Puppies smell good to me too," he said. "But I expect your mommas would prefer for you to smell more like that soap and less like those dogs when you get home."

"My momma starts sneezing when I come home after I've been playing with dogs," Johnny said. "That's why I can't have one. Dogs and cats make her sneeze. The mule don't though."

"Wash extra good then," Ukiah said. "I sure wouldn't want your momma mad at me 'cause you were making her sneeze."

The children lathered up good, finally completing the cleaning process when Ukiah dumped the bucket of water over them rinsing the suds off.

"As good as if you were headed to Sunday church," he pronounced. "Y'all come back and visit when you like. You too, Johnny."

The kids had almost made it back to the path going down the hill when Ukiah yelled at them.

"Hold up!"

He came up with a burlap sack with something rattling around inside of it. He opened the bag and showed them two jars of moonshine.

"Would you mind dropping these off at Miss Callie's?"

"Sure," Caleb said, reaching for the sack.

"Now if anybody asks what you've got in the sack, don't say anything and just show them a jar of the syrup," he said, taking the jars from each of them and putting them in the sack. "That way you wouldn't be lying and it might help avoid any embarrassing questions. You understand don't you?"

He winked at Caleb, who winked back.

"Yes'sir," Caleb said, although he really didn't.

34

CHAPTER 6

Miss Callie

The kids made their way back down the hill and wandered through camp on their way to Miss Callie's house which was plain, neat in appearance, and set a little ways off from the rest of the camp, behind a stand of cane which blocked it from the view of the other houses. A well worn trail led to the cabin and the children passed Mr. Jones, one of the carpenters, on the path leaving the house.

"Howdy Mr. Jones," Caleb said as they passed.

"Hi," he received in return, the man lowering his head and hurrying away.

"That's weird," Caleb said. "He's usually real talkative."

The kids knew that the ways of adults were strange and there was no real discussion of the matter as they continued on to their destination.

As was usual at all the houses in the camp, the wooden front door was open and the screen door was closed, the dog trot style houses designed to stay as cool as possible in the hot Louisiana weather.

Caleb knocked on the frame of the screen door, feeling it rattle under the pressure.

"Miss Callie?" he called. "It's me, Caleb Gandy."

"Just a moment," he heard a woman's voice call out from the back of the house.

In a minute or two a pretty young, blonde woman appeared, her hair up in a bun she was fiddling with as she approached the door.

"Hello Caleb. It's a pleasure to see you. How are you doing?" she asked as she opened the door.

"I'm fine," he said politely. Miss Callie was so pretty she always made him a little tongue tied.

"Hello Leesie," she said. "And who is this fine fellow?"

"This is Johnny Robinson ma'am. He's Miss Gaskey's grandson and his daddy just started to work in the camp."

"Well I'm pleased to meet you, Johnny Robinson," Miss Callie curtsied as she said this. "Would you kids like some tea?"

"Yes'm. That'd be good."

Southern hospitality required that a visit to someone's home required the offer and acceptance of food and drink. Caleb and Leesie had been taught this from a young age and Johnny followed their lead.

Miss Callie brought a tray with a pitcher of sweet tea and a few cookies on a plate. Each child politely took one but Caleb and Leesie quickly stuffed theirs in their pockets when she turned away. While Miss Callie was pretty, it was widely known she couldn't cook a lick. Johnny ate his cookie, but with a noticeable lack of gusto.

"So, to what do I owe the honor of this visit?" She asked after the drinks were finished and the cookies had disappeared.

"Ukiah asked us to deliver this to you," Caleb said, removing the three jars of syrup and handing the bag to her.

She took the bag and looked inside.

"Just so you know, this isn't for me, it's for...friends...who come by. I don't drink myself."

"Yes'm," Caleb said, Leesie nodding and Johnny still trying to choke down the last bite of his cookie.

As she was talking, Miss Callie had absent mindedly pulled a small, silver watch from a pocket on the front of her dress and was fiddling with the long, shiny braided cord attached to the top of it. She flipped it open and shut a few times, drifting away in thought as she looked at Leesie.

She suddenly seemed to remember she had guests and snapped the watch open.

"Have I ever showed you a picture of my daughter?" she asked Leesie.

"No ma'am."

She passed the watch to Leesie. On the inside of the cover, opposite the watch face was a small picture of a girl, slightly younger than Leesie but very similar in appearance.

"That watch belonged to her father, the cord is made from her hair."

"She's pretty," Leesie said. "Where is she?"

"She's with my parents in Alabama. After her daddy left I fell on some hard times. I didn't want Elizabeth, that's her name, to see me like this so I sent her home to my parents until I could get enough money saved up to take care of her."

"Do you miss her?" Leesie asked.

"Lots. But...," as she said this, her face broke into a smile, "I almost have enough money saved now where I can afford to go home and open a little business and take care of us. Maybe a store, or maybe a laundry like your mom, Leesie."

Caleb wasn't sure how Miss Callie had managed to save money, because she didn't have a job as far as Caleb knew and she was always wearing new dresses. That may be the reason she wasn't invited to the quilting bees or the other things the women of the camp got together to do. Come to think of it, Caleb had never seen her on any of the church committees either.

"So you're going to be moving?" Caleb asked.

"Yes'sir. In a couple of months I'm going to light a shuck for Natchitoches and catch a train to Alabama. I'll start over and nobody will know what I've done or look down on me anymore."

The kids understood little of what she was

37

saying, but nodded anyway. They did understand that she was leaving.

"Leesie, I know you play with dolls, why don't you stop by in a few days and I'll give you some doll clothes I don't feel like taking all the way to Alabama."

Just then the watch sitting on the table began playing the tune "London Bridge".

Leesie giggled and picked it up.

"You like that? That's my daughter's favorite song. When her daddy heard that watch sound off on the hour with it he just had to have it."

"I've never heard a pocket watch play a song before," Caleb said.

"Neither had I, but the man he bought it from said it was made special in Switzerland. It cost nearly ten dollars."

The children oohed and aahed over the watch, then took their leave and headed home. Before they left Miss Callie promised to write them and let them know she had made it to Alabama all right.

As they were walking through camp Caleb saw his daddy sitting on a stump outside of the barber shop and they wandered that way.

"Hey Daddy," Caleb said.

"Well, if it's not triple trouble. What have you three been up to today?"

"We went up to Ukiah's to introduce Johnny."

"Oh, you did? Didn't bother to check on any dogs while you were up there did you?"

"Sure did. Queenie had her litter. Ukiah said I could take Bo home in six or seven weeks."

"Bo, huh? Already named him have you?"

"Sure have. I'm not sure which one he is yet, but I know his name is Bo. That just sounds like the name of a good dog."

"That it does. It surely does. What do you have there?" He pointed toward the jars the kids were carrying.

"Ukiah gave us each a jar of syrup for helping

38

him grind cane."

"That was nice of him. Did you thank him proper?"

"Yes sir."

"I'm curious though. If you came from Ukiah's, who lives over there," he pointed in the direction of Ukiah's cabin, "what are you doing coming from that direction?" This time he pointed toward Miss Callie's. "Were you wandering a bit?"

"No sir. Ukiah asked us to take a couple of jars to Miss Callie."

Caleb didn't bother to volunteer that it wasn't syrup they'd delivered. Leesie and Johnny stayed quiet, their loyalty to Caleb stronger than any loyalty to telling the complete truth.

"What a Saturday. A moonshiner and a woman of ill repu...," Mr. Gandy stopped in mid-sentence, remembering the kids were there. "I know lots of grown men who don't have that good of a Saturday."

Caleb didn't know how to respond, so didn't say anything.

His daddy looked thoughtful for a second.

"I'll tell you something though. It might be a good idea if y'all didn't mention the trip to Miss Callie's to anybody else, all right? Particularly not your mother."

The children nodded in agreement, not sure why but sensing Mr. Gandy understood adults better than they would.

CHAPTER 7

Bo

Caleb spent a lot of time at Ukiah's over the next six weeks, sometimes with Johnny and Leesie and sometimes without. His dad gave him a small notebook in which he kept meticulous notes on each of the eight puppies, evaluating them for their coloring, appearance, rambunctiousness, and other factors known only to him. Each night he discussed the pros and cons of each with his father, who listened patiently and occasionally asked questions to let Caleb know he was paying attention.

However, in his heart Caleb had already made his choice, the identity of Bo being established almost immediately after the puppies started walking. He had watched the largest male pup carefully track a caterpillar, bowl over two sisters and a brother, and then pounce clumsily but happily into his lap and proceed to give his face a lick bath. His heart and the name were immediately bestowed on the floppy eared puppy.

Nevertheless, Caleb espoused that he was keeping an open mind even though a review of his notes would have shown that Bo had no cons, but lots of pros. He'd studied Bo's tracking abilities, carefully listing each critter tracked, whether it be bug, chicken, other dog, or whatever, the length of time tracked, and whether or not Bo ever gave up on the hunt without being forced to do so due to assault by other puppies or being scooped up by Caleb.

When they accompanied him, Leesie and Johnny would quickly grow bored with Caleb's studies and wander off to other endeavors, but Caleb had a single minded focus, only stopping long enough to eat lunch, which he did with a squirming puppy on his lap frequently trying and succeeding in taking food from his hand.

It was obvious from watching Bo that he had made his choice as well. When Caleb arrived, Bo would break into an awkward, stumbling run at the first sight or smell of the boy.

While he would occasionally leave Caleb's side to harass a littermate or some other puppy adventure, he'd look over every few minutes to make sure his boy was still there. Occasionally he'd lose sight, but his wonderful nose would quickly find Caleb no matter where he was.

Ukiah told him that every time Caleb left he'd have to tie Bo up near his mom or the dog would try to follow the boy back to camp.

The instincts of the dogs really showed through on the day that Caleb brought a raccoon tail to the yard and ran around dragging it on a string. When he released the puppies from their confinement in the barn, the bedlam commenced as soon as each dog caught the scent and started trying to track the drag, tumbling over each other and making their first attempts at what would one day be melodious baying but which was, for now, just yips, yaps, and a general racket. Occasionally one of the pups would get distracted and abandon the chase, but Bo stayed focused other than when he mistakenly put a cat up a tree, looked baffled for a moment, then lowered his nose to the ground and cast back and forth before picking up the scent and continuing his tracking.

Eventually Caleb threw the raccoon tail into the midst of the mass of puppies and watched as the fighting and tussling over the severed appendage commenced. After a minute or so Bo shot out from the pile with the tail firmly grasped in his puppy teeth, running this way and that, dodging the rest of his litter

41

before finally reaching a place of refuge and safety behind Caleb's legs. The boy picked him up and held him and the prize out of the reach of the rest of the dogs. Queenie raised her head from her prone position on the porch to see what was causing all of the commotion, then lowered it and went back to sleep, seemingly glad that the litter had their attention focused somewhere other than on her.

Ukiah stood to one side, laughing at the ruckus.

"I guess that's Bo?" he asked Caleb.

The boy had thought he would sit with Ukiah and debate the selection of the dog, but found he couldn't deny his heart for even that length of time.

"This is Bo," he replied.

Ukiah reached in his back pocket and removed an object, throwing it to Caleb, who caught it with his free hand, the wiggling puppy, raccoon tail still clenched in his teeth, tucked under the other arm.

It was a leather collar with a small brass plate attached to it. "My name is Bo. I belong to Caleb Gandy" was scratched neatly into the brass.

"Thanks Ukiah," Caleb said, taking the raccoon tail from his dog and throwing it a few feet to the side, drawing the rest of the noisy litter away from him.

He flopped to the ground and began trying to put the collar on the puppy, who was desperately struggling to get away and back to the tail which was again the subject of a brawl.

After much scratching and struggling on the part of the dog and the boy, the collar was finally put on Bo, who used his hind leg to scratch at it for a minute, then promptly ignored it.

"A mite big", Ukiah said. "But I figure he's got some growing to do."

"I imagine so."

"Are you ready to take him home and let him meet your parents?"

"Sure! You mean he can start living with me?"

"Sure can. Some of the buyers for the rest of the

pups will start coming this week, and I imagine he'll get pretty lonely on this hill without them around. Grab yourself a piece of rope to use for a leash and take him to his new house."

Bo, however, had other ideas about the whole leash business. At first he would grab whatever piece of rope was dangling and play tug of war with Caleb as long as possible. Then, when Caleb wasn't paying attention for a minute, Bo grabbed the rope away from him and a chase was required to get it back. Finally, after he finished laughing and caught his breath, Ukiah brought a biscuit from the house and fed it to Bo a small piece at a time while Caleb tied the rope onto the collar.

Everything was fine until Bo felt the leash tighten. At that moment he changed from a coon dog into a caterwauling plow. Rather than walking with Caleb, the leash loose between them, Bo planted his feet and refused to move of his own volition. Caleb dragged him about ten feet, then stopped and scratched his head.

"He sure doesn't like being tied does he?" Ukiah asked.

"Sure doesn't."

"He likes following you well enough, why don't you drop your end of the leash and let it drag behind him? Give him a chance to get used to feeling a little pressure on it."

Caleb shrugged.

"Sounds like a good idea."

Caleb made his way down the hill, Bo a few feet behind him, occasionally looking over his shoulder as if surprised Ukiah wasn't making him stay there. They had to stop several times on their trek back to camp to untangle the rope from where it had gotten hung up on briars or roots. Eventually, Bo allowed Caleb to carry the other end as long as he didn't put any pressure on it. This meant their route meandered quite a bit since Bo constantly left the trail to sniff around and explore.

43

Caleb was hoping there'd be a lot of people stirring around camp so he'd have a chance to show off his dog, and he wasn't disappointed.

"Howdy Caleb. Fine looking dog you've got there," Mr. Lumpkin yelled across at him when they passed an open area where a bunch of the older men had gathered to whittle, chew tobacco, and tell stories.

"Thanks Mr. Lumpkin."

"Gonna teach him how to hunt?"

"I expect so."

"Won't be a coon safe in Kisatchie Forest," one of the other men observed and they all laughed, remembering the way they roamed the forest in their youth.

Caleb was most happy when he came across a gang of his school chums, walking with fishing poles slung over their shoulders.

"Hey Caleb!" Willy Lee yelled at him. "Want to come fishing with us?"

"Can't!" he yelled back. "Got to start training my dog!"

The boys swerved from their path and gathered around Caleb and Bo.

"What kind is he?" Joe Lee, Will's brother, asked.

"Genuine full blooded Blue Tick Hound."

"Where'd you get him?" This one was from Luke Elmore.

"Ukiah. He was the pick of the litter."

"He's sure a beaut. What'cha gonna train him to do?"

"'Coon huntin' of course. Although I 'spect we'll do our share of squirrel hunting too. I don't think I'll let him run deer. He's too valuable," Caleb said importantly.

"Aw, he don't look like all that much," Tommy Sanders said. "Just looks like an old half breed hound."

Caleb balled up the fist not holding Bo's leash and was about to challenge Tommy when Joe busted in.

44

"Are you kidding? Everybody knows old Ukiah sells his dogs for more than a mule costs. How much is your dog worth Tommy? Even if he wasn't eat up with the mange."

That shut the other boy up without the need for Caleb to administer a whoopin' and was more than satisfactory. Caleb noticed that even Ben Johnson looked impressed, and spent a long time scratching Bo behind his ears.

Eventually the band of boys moved on to their rendezvous with the creek, several of them whistling at Bo and patting their legs to try and get him to follow them, but the pup was content to sit at Caleb's feet, showing no interest in the other boys once they moved beyond Caleb's vicinity.

Leesie was playing in her yard when the two approached.

"Oh Caleb, I knew this one was Bo," she said, grabbing the puppy and holding him close to her chest. "I could tell by the way you looked at each other."

"Yup, he was the best of the bunch."

"I think so too. He's perfect."

Caleb agreed.

Life had been good before, but now that he had his dog, life was pretty near perfect.

CHAPTER 8

Training Bo

"Johnny! You're going to have to run faster than that, Bo'll catch you in no time!"

"I can't run no faster, Caleb," Johnny said, bending over and breathing hard, the pelt of a recently killed racoon tied to the end of a string running from his belt. "The skin keeps gettin' hung up on stuff."

He yanked on the string to show that the drag was, even now, tangled in more briars.

Caleb flopped down on the path and put his hands on his cheeks to think.

"We need a real 'coon, but I don't see how that's likely to happen."

He thought some more.

"So if we can't get a real coon, then we have to use the skin and a fake coon to lay the trail, right?"

Johnny nodded in agreement.

"We already know you're too slow, and Leesie's even slower than you are. I can't do it because I've got to work Bo."

"What about one of your t'other friends?" Johnny asked hesitantly. He was still afraid that if Caleb's other friends were around he wouldn't be welcome.

"Nah, you're the fastest kid around and besides, I wouldn't trust none of them to help with Bo." He didn't notice how Johnny's face lit up when he said this. Nobody other than his parents, and particularly nobody white, had ever trusted him to do anything. The best he ever hoped for was to remain unnoticed and undisturbed.

Bo was at Leesie's now, tied to a tree in her yard and kept mollified by Leesie's attention and the table scraps she fed him. Caleb had left her with strict instructions about the dog's care. He had been mortified once when he'd returned from a fishing trip with his dad to find Leesie had tied ribbons around Bo's neck, attire entirely unbecoming what was sure to be the greatest 'coon dog in the history of Louisiana.

"We need a real coon. They can run fast, duck in and out of brush piles and tight places and climb trees."

He continued thinking and absent mindedly scratched the ears of one of Mrs. Finstrom's cats that had wandered up and began rubbing against him.

Johnny unhooked the coon skin from his leg and began teasing the cat with it, flipping it in front of him then dragging it back trying to get the cat to follow it. The cat was less than enamored with the process and would half-heartedly grab at it but not with the usual cat intensity.

Eventually, Caleb started watching the game between his friend and the cat, wondering why the cat wasn't more interested. Johnny's next throw landed the skin on top of the cat, who immediately started bucking and spitting until the hateful thing was dislodged.

Johnny and Caleb look at each other and smiled.

Some ingenuity, some more string, and a couple of dozen claw marks later, the boys had a reasonable facsimile of a raccoon, if raccoons hissed and spat and meowed loudly and as if in pain.

"That'll work," Caleb said, inspecting their project which Johnny was holding at arm's length, dodging all four legs and the arsenal attached to them as much as possible.

Caleb ran to Leesie's and untied Bo from the tree, grabbing the end of the leash and holding on as Bo went through the normal minute or so of gymnastics before settling in and accepting the notion that the leash wasn't going anywhere. Leesie followed the two back to where Johnny continued dancing around, mostly avoiding the clawing attempts by the enraged cat. The feline's frantic activities increased exponentially when it saw Bo, who was already the most hated dog among the camp's cat community.

As Bo lunged, Caleb dropped to his knees and put the dog in a headlock, both he and the hound rocking back and forth as he struggled to free himself and get to the cat, which was flopping around and making lots of noise as Johnny continued to dodge the flailing limbs and claws.

"Oh, be careful," Leesie said. "Don't hurt the poor thing!"

"Him...or...me?" Johnny asked, ducking and narrowly missing a raking across the cheek.

"When...I...say...go...," Caleb said, grunting the words out between Bo's leaps forward and backward. "You...chunk...the...cat...toward...the...woods...I'll...give...him...a...head...start...then...let...Bo...go...Oops!"

Bo had given a healthy leap backwards, changing both tactics and direction, and his head popped from between Caleb's arms. With a leap, Bo hit Johnny. Unfortunately for the boy, the cat was on a pendulum swing toward him at that instant and the extra momentum enabled him to get four good claw holds on Johnny at the exact instant the boy's grip relaxed. The cat did as cats do when confronted with danger from below.

He climbed up.

For a few seconds the sight would have been comical to anyone watching who didn't have a vested interest in dog, friend, cat, or skin, but none of the participants laughed. The cat perched on top of Johnny's head, back arched and every hair that could be seen standing on end. The cat hissed, Johnny yelled, and Bo barked furiously as he tried to climb Johnny as well, although he only succeeded in knocking the boy backward.

When the cat realized that his proximity to the dog was still too close he leapt down and took off running toward the woods, immediately followed by the dog, who was not able to catch up because he kept tripping over the leash.

Caleb missed his dive to grab the rope and now ran after the dog, followed closely by Johnny and Leesie, although Johnny was slower than usual as he spent part of his energy inspecting himself for any serious, cat related injuries.

All three of the kids dove at the leash at different times during the chase, although it was rare that they got close enough to have a real shot at grabbing it. All they had to show for their endeavors were scratches and scrapes as the leash stayed out of their grasps.

From the sounds, Bo caught the cat at least once in a brush pile but since the cat shot out the other side still at the same pace as when the chase had begun, Caleb assumed the raccoon fur which was still attached had protected him from Bo.

"We've got to grab him, this isn't doing any good, he's not tracking he's just chasing!" Caleb yelled.

The chase continued through a stand of trees, the cat, apparently disillusioned with his last vertical venture, ignoring the opportunity to climb in favor of continuing at a full out run.

Leesie managed to get her hands on Bo's leash once, but her grip was broken when he dragged her a couple of feet. She managed to slow him enough for Johnny and Caleb to nearly catch up, and for the cat to stretch its lead.

The next clearing had several brush piles in it and Bo seemed to be having a hard time figuring out where the cat was. He narrowed it down to two mounds and was running back and forth between them baying when the kids hit the clearing. When the dog saw them he realized he was about to be grabbed and launched himself into the biggest pile.

"I'll go in and try to grab the leash and drag him out. If he comes out without me, you two grab him and hold on," Caleb said.

Leesie and Johnny took their places on opposite sides of the brush pile. They could hear both Caleb and the dog moving around inside the huge pile of branches and sticks. Even though it was nearly 30 feet around, they could still see the pile shaking and hear Caleb swearing as he was poked or scratched by some portion of the pile.

"Caleb," Leesie yelled. "You watch out for snakes."

One part of the pile, apparently where Caleb was located, abruptly stopped shaking, even though another part, presumably where Bo was located, continued to shake and emit howls.

"You reckon there's snakes in here?" Caleb's voice came from the pile.

"Not for long," Johnny said.

The pile began shaking again, the movements getting closer together as Caleb started giving a running commentary.

"Gosh it's hot in here. Lots of pointy things too."

Shake shake.

"I can see Bo now, it looks like he's almost got him. Don't see the leash though."

Leesie caught a flash out of the corner of her eye and turned to see the cat running from the other brush pile in the direction of the camp.

"Uh, Caleb..."

"Hush Leesie. It's dark in here too. Dang it! My shirt's caught!"

They heard the sound of ripping cloth.

"I'm fine now."

"Caleb, I think I just..."

Caleb cut her off again.

"Hush Leesie. Y'all listen and I'll let you know when to grab him."

The shaking moved a little more toward the end where the sound of the dog could be heard.

"I'm almost up to him. Come on Bo! Let's go!"

This was followed by some more swear words.

"Dang it! He's not listening and I can't get a grip on him in here. I'm going to try and poke the cat out with a stick. When Bo chases him out y'all get ready and grab him."

The sound of a stick banging against other sticks could be heard, then Caleb began yelling encouragement to his dog.

"Get him Bo! Get him! That's the way boy, get him!"

The brush pile started shaking frantically and Bo's baying increased in both enthusiasm and volume.

"Say Johnny, what color was that cat?" Caleb yelled out.

"Grayish brown. Same color as that coon skin," Johnny yelled back.

"That's funny it looks kind of black and white in here. I wonder…OH NO! NO BO, NO! STOP! STOP! GET AWAY FROM THERE. COME HERE BO, COME HERE!"

The shaking threatened to shake the brush pile apart, and Leesie and Johnny could see Caleb forcing his way up through the sticks and branches rather than back out one of the tunnels.

Occasionally he'd lurch upward, still yelling at the dog.

"NO BO! NO! PLEASE LEAVE HIM ALONE BO!"

Just then Caleb's voice was obscured by what sounded like gagging, just about the same time Bo's barking changed to a surprised howl. The shaking increased again and from the changing positions of the sounds it was apparent both Caleb and Bo were on the move.

"NO BO! STOP! GET AWAY FROM ME! GET AWAY FROM ME BO! OH BO!"

51

The reason for the change in both attitude and direction became apparent when an overwhelming stench wafted out from the brush pile, engulfing both Leesie and Johnny.

"Whew!" Johnny cried, holding his nose. "I think Bo got confused on his cats!"

"Yeah," Leeise said. "He found a pole cat instead of a house cat." She giggled around the fingers holding her nose closed.

Caleb tumbled backward out of the same hole he had entered, followed a second later by Bo who erupted as well. The dog landed on top of Caleb and frantically began wiping his muzzle and eyes on the boy, until he pushed him to the side at which point Bo put his nose on the ground and began wiping it with his front paws.

"Oh Bo! What'd you do?" Caleb got up from the ground and ran over to where Leesie and Johnny were standing, laughing.

"It's not funny y'all. Let's get out of here before he gets any more on us."

Johnny took his fingers off his nose and sniffed quickly, then clamped them back in place.

"I believe it's a little late for one of us," he said, backing away from Caleb as Leesie did the same.

"Oh come on guys! What are we gonna do?"

"We're going home," Leesie said. "But I 'spect you're going to be doing a lot of dog washing for a week or two."

As she said this Bo, still floundering around nearly blinded by the skunk spray, ran into the back of Caleb's legs and knocked him to the ground, then rolled back and forth trying to get out from under the boy. It was a dejected looking boy and dog who made their way back into camp, trailing well behind Leesie and Johnny who would occasionally turn and warn them to stay back.

Caleb and Bo made a detour to the creek a ways downstream from the camp, but when he started scrubbing the stench just got stronger. Leesie came running up with a bar of strong, lye soap and threw it to Caleb.

"Your momma said try this," she said, holding her nose and running off giggling.

The soap didn't appear to make much difference.

"Well, I guess there is probably a lesson to be learned from this, but I'm not sure what it is." His daddy's voice came from just over the top of the creek bank.

Caleb's face was full of suds, but after he washed them off he saw his daddy sitting on a log, smiling but not laughing. At his feet were a number of large, silver cans. He grabbed one, punched holes in the top of it with his knife, and then leaned down and handed it to Caleb, holding his nose shut with the fingers of the other hand.

"Mr. Jenkins said that tomato juice works better on skunk smell than anything he knows of, although nothing would make it all go away. Still, some help is better than none. You better drag that skunk dog up on the bank and get to scrubbing. Use the first three or four cans on him, the use the rest on you."

"You gonna help, Daddy?"

"I would son, but when the same thing happened to me and my hound, my daddy told me there's just some things a man has got to do for himself. This is one of them. No need for all the menfolk in the Gandy house to stink."

He stood up and motioned toward some clothes on the log next to him.

"Your momma sent these for you to change into, and asked me to tell you to drop your skunk bit ones off at Miss Osborne's to see what she can do to get the smell out. If'n she can't, just tell her to burn them and that we'll pay her for her efforts either way. And when you get home don't dare bring that dog inside. Your ma is fixing a pallet for you and him to sleep on the back porch. I expect that'll be your room for at least a week or two."

His daddy smiled again and jumped back as Bo shook himself just after Caleb applied the first dose of tomato juice, peppering Caleb from head to toe with the liquid.

"Rub it in good, let it soak for a while, then rinse it off. Keep doing that until you run out and I'll see you at the house."

He turned to leave, took a few steps, then stopped and turned back.

"By the way, do you know who stopped me on the way over here?" he asked Caleb.

"No sir," he said, although he had a feeling he might.

"Mrs. Finstrom. It appears somebody tied a 'coon skin around her cat. The poor thing is sitting on the porch just twitching and shaking. I allowed as to how it might have just found that old skin and gotten tangled up in it. She said she didn't believe it could have tangled itself into knots quite that good, but said as long as it didn't happen again she figured my explanation was as good as any. I imagine it would be impossible for that to happen again, don't you?"

"I think you're right. It'd surprise me if it *ever* happened again."

"That's what I thought."

Mr. Gandy took a few more steps toward home and stopped again.

"How did he sound when he opened up on the chase?"

"Wonderful, Daddy. He sounded great."

For the next few weeks they slept on the porch each night, his daddy coming out to smoke his pipe and tell stories. Those nights would remain some of Caleb's best memories, him sitting there with Bo snuggled up against him, his daddy's voice and the smell of his tobacco mingled with the gradually fading odor of skunk.

54

Although the smell faded with time, for months whenever Bo got wet the scent of the skunk would waft from him. The memories of those nights on the back porch would last as long as Caleb did.

CHAPTER 9

A Disappearance from the Camp

"So what do y'all want to do today?" Caleb asked on a day when the three friends were gathered at his house.

"I'm always doing boy stuff with y'all, how about you play dolls with me for a little while?"

Caleb looked at Johnny, who looked back.

"Now that I think about it," Caleb said. "I believe I'm coming down with something." He worked up a couple of fake coughs.

Johnny copied him.

Leesie stomped her foot.

"That's not fair," she said.

"Fair or not, I'm not playing with dolls. Cowboys and Indians?"

"Nope," Leesie said, lower lip stuck out in a pout.

"Fishing?"

"Uh uh."

"Well, what *do* you want to do?" Caleb asked. "Other than playing with dolls."

Leesie thought for a minute. "We could go to Miss Callie's and get those doll clothes she promised me."

Caleb looked at Johnny, who shrugged.

"I guess that'd be okay. But let's not stay long and maybe we can avoid having to eat any of her cookies."

The kids, with Bo tagging along of course, made their way back down the trail to Miss Callie's house.

This time they didn't meet anybody on their trek.

The flower gardens out front were wilted.

Caleb hopped up on the porch and knocked on the screen door, which was ajar.

"Miss Callie?"

No response from inside the house.

He knocked again.

"Miss Callie? It's Caleb Gandy. Are you here?"

Still quiet.

Leesie tapped on the door.

"Miss Callie, it's Leesie Osborne. I came by to get those doll clothes you said I could have."

"Maybe she's in the outhouse," Johnny offered.

Caleb stepped around the side of the house, reappearing a moment later.

"Nope, not there either."

Leesie had the door open and Johnny was looking over her shoulder into the living room where they had visited and had cookies last time.

"Oooo whee, it sho' do look to' up in there," he said.

Caleb pushed Leesie on into the room, Johnny following behind her.

The table where the cookies had sat was overturned, the glass decorations smashed on the floor along with a quart jar like the ones the kids had brought from Ukiah's.

"I think we'd better go get my daddy," Caleb said.

They found Mr. Gandy sitting on the front porch of Mr. Jenkin's store with several other men, eating their lunches and talking.

"Daddy, come quick," Caleb said as he ran up.

"Whoa! Whoa now! Take it easy." His dad took a sip of coffee from his cup and sat his sandwich down on the towel it had been wrapped in.

"What's up?" he asked.

"We were just at Miss Callie's picking up some doll clothes for Leesie and we think something may

57

have happened to her."

"What makes you believe that?"

"Her door was open and the living room is all tore up," Leesie offered.

Mr. Gandy stood as the men started putting their lunches back in the pails they carried them in.

"We'd better go take a look," he said.

The group made their way to the house, the other men from the porch falling in behind them.

"Y'all wait out here," Mr. Gandy told them. "Bob, John," he indicated two of the men. "Come with me."

Two men separated from the pack and followed him into the house. All three returned a few minutes later.

"Caleb, run to the store and tell Mr. Jenkins to call the sheriff and ask him to come out."

The lawman couldn't make it until the next day, when he arrived in a truck, bouncing his way down the rutted road leading to camp. As usual, all the kids gathered around any vehicle that appeared, since they were still a novelty in that part of the country. He parked at the store.

"Y'all stay here," Mr. Gandy told the kids. "The sheriff will want to talk to you later on. For now, go inside and tell Mr. Jenkins I said you could have soda pops on me."

Caleb turned to say something to Johnny, but was greeted by the sight of the screen door slamming shut as the other boy darted into the store. Caleb and Leesie quickly followed, Bo flopping down on the porch after being stopped by the screen door closing in his face.

"Howdy, Mr. Jenkins," Caleb said. Leesie curtsied and Johnny waved at the storekeeper. "Daddy said for us to get three soda pops and put them on his bill, if that's all right."

"That'd be fine," Mr. Jenkins replied. "Help yourselves to a cookie from the jar too. Compliments of the house."

This time Johnny chose an orange soda (That sho' is a pretty color, he exclaimed), while Caleb and Leesie both got a Coca-Cola. Mr. Jenkins popped the top on an orange soda for himself and joined the kids sitting on the front porch.

Caleb broke off a piece of his cookie and shared with Bo, who then visited Leesie and Johnny for their contribution before sitting expectantly in front of Mr. Jenkins. After a few minutes of unabated staring, Mr. Jenkins mumbled, "Oh, all right," and gave Bo the rest of his cookie, which Bo gulped down and then thanked him by giving him a sloppy lick on his hand.

Ed Latham strolled up that minute and climbed the steps to the porch of the store.

"I need some supplies," he told Mr. Jenkins, ignoring the kids. Bo's hackles rose slightly and Caleb could hear a low growl coming from him.

"You're paid up so pick out what you need and put it on the counter, Ed. I'll be in directly."

The door closed behind Latham as he entered the store.

"Yes'sir, walked in and paid his bill in full, just like he used to. Maybe old Ed's turned a corner and give up wasting all his money on hooch," Mr. Jenkins said quietly, then continued in a conversational tone. "I didn't notice that Miss Callie hadn't been around in a few days. She was in here on Tuesday and your daddy," he indicated Johnny by pointing the soda bottle at him, "helped her carry her stuff home, but I usually see her every other day. She's always such a pleasure to visit with. I hope she's all right."

"Yes sir, she's nice," Caleb agreed and Leesie nodded her head. Johnny kind of bobbed his, but didn't take his mouth off of the top of the soda bottle.

After a few minutes of pleasant talk Mr. Jenkins disappeared into the store to take care of Mr. Latham, who reappeared several minutes later with his arms full of packages and supplies. He walked past the kids without acknowledging them in any way.

It was a while before the sheriff and the rest of the men made their way back to the store, a grim faced Mr. Gandy walking next to the lawman.

"The kids went by there to pick up some doll clothes Callie had for Leesie," he explained to the other man.

"Did y'all touch anything in the house?" the sheriff asked.

"No sir."

Caleb was awestruck to be speaking to a real, sure enough sheriff. Leesie and Johnny stayed quiet, but the size of Johnny's eyes indicated his impression of the man. He was staring at the revolver strapped to the lawman's right hip.

"When was the last time you talked to Miss Callie?"

"About two weeks ago. That's when she told us she was going back to Alabama and that Leesie could have a bunch of doll clothes."

"Did she say when she was leaving?"

Caleb thought for a moment, but Leesie answered before he could.

"No sir. She just said she'd saved her money and was going soon."

The sheriff tilted his hat back and wiped his forehead with a blue gingham handkerchief he pulled from his pocket.

"It just doesn't make any sense that she would leave all her clothes and stuff behind. Plus, how would she get out of camp without anybody knowing? She sure wasn't going to walk all the way to Natchitoches."

Mr. Jenkins appeared with a cold bottle of soda he handed to the sheriff, who nodded in thanks and downed half the bottle in a gulp, letting out a big belch followed by a small "excuse me".

"Thanks," he said to Mr. Jenkins. "That sure hit the spot. Say, does Miss Callie have an account here?"

"She sure does. She's always ordering dresses

and such. Groceries too, of course."

"Is it paid up?"

The storekeeper didn't even have to look at the books to answer.

"No sir, she owes for this month. About five dollars or so."

"Did she mention anything about leaving? Moving to Alabama?"

"She was always talking about going home and getting her daughter, but she wouldn't have left without settling up with me and saying her good-byes around camp. She wasn't like that."

"When's the last time you saw her?"

"She was in here on Tuesday, just before dark. She bought a slab of bacon, a big sack of flour, and several cans of peaches. She loved canned peaches. Luther Robinson carried her stuff for her."

"I'll need to talk to him then, is he around?" the sheriff asked Mr. Gandy, who turned to one of the men.

"Lester, Luther's down by Loblolly Creek. Take my horse, go down there and relieve him and send him back on the horse. Don't mention what it's about to anybody, just tell him I need to see him."

The man took off at a fast walk in the direction of the corral.

"Does Miss Callie have a particular boyfriend?" The Sheriff asked.

The men looked at each other, some of them shifting uncomfortably from foot to foot.

Mr. Gandy cleared his throat, then looked at the Sheriff.

"If you're finished with the young 'uns this would probably be a good time for them to go home."

Caleb saw him raise his eyebrows at the lawman.

"Of course. I can ask them more later if it is necessary."

"Kids, y'all go to the house. I expect Luther will be tied up for a while so Johnny can eat with us and I'll send somebody to tell Dora they'll be late."

"Yes sir."

The men stayed silent until the kids were on their way. Behind them, Caleb could hear the talking start up again.

Well after dark Luther Robinson, looking worried, stopped by the house and picked Johnny up on the way home. Not long after that Mr. Gandy arrived, ate supper alone at the kitchen table, and then shooed Caleb and Bo off to their room for the night, shutting the door behind them.

Caleb slipped out of bed and cracked his window, then knelt next to it where he could hear his mother and father talking on the back porch.

"We found a few scraps of lace and fabric caught up on one of the bushes along the trail behind Callie's house, but it was a good quarter mile away. Not likely she'd have been strolling along that path."

"Are you sure it was her's?"

"Dan Jenkins is. He said it was some lace he'd special ordered for Callie about two months ago. We went through her closet and found some more just like it."

"What do you think happened?"

"I have no idea, but it can't be good. I'd like to think she went home to Alabama but her closet is stuffed full, she didn't pay her bill at the store, and no one saw her leave. Plus, she didn't own a wagon or horse, so how would she get anywhere? If someone gave her a lift, she'd have been seen or someone would have said so."

"No one knows anything?"

"Luther Robinson helped her carry some groceries home on Tuesday night after work and he said she was fine and everything looked all right. He said she offered him something to eat but he turned her down and went on home. Of course, it looks bad that Luther was the last man seen with her, particularly since he's colored. Ed Latham started mouthing off

62

about that as soon as Luther showed up, talking about niggers and white women. The Sheriff finally shut him up but I could hear some grumbling and whispering among the men. I'll have to keep an eye on things for a while."

"Surely no one thinks Luther did anything? He's gentle as a lamb."

"You know how ignorant some people are. They want someone to blame and Luther makes a good target. Add to that the fact that Luther's doing a 'white man's job' and you suddenly have an uppity nigger in some folk's minds and things can get out of hand. It was just a couple of years ago they hung that black fellow up in Campti for murdering a white woman only to find out later she'd run off with a railroad man."

"Could things like that happen here? These are good people."

"Most of them are, but even good people sometimes do bad or stupid things. It's just human nature. If Ed will keep his mouth shut things should settle down."

"Is that likely?"

"Not with Ed. You know how he is. Maybe Callie will show back up and this whole thing will blow over."

The conversation changed to general camp talk and Caleb closed the window and slipped back into bed, Bo right behind him.

CHAPTER 10

Hunting Hogs

"I don't 'spect I'm gonna have much time for playin' or schoolin' for a while," Johnnie replied one day when Leesie asked him if he was ready to start learning his letters.

"Why not?"

"Poppa said our mule is getting on poorly and we're gonna have to get another one. He knows where he can get one for fifty dollars, but that's a heap of money and so we're gonna have to plant some more ground and take on some extra jobs to pay for it."

Caleb was sitting on the ground near them, pulling on Bo's tail to annoy him while the dog happily gnawed on a bone. Occasionally, Bo would growl a little and turn to gnaw and slobber on Caleb's hand until the boy let go of his tail, when he'd return his attention to the bone and the boy would grab his tail again.

"I know how we could earn some money," Caleb said.

"How's that?" Leesie asked suspiciously. Often, Caleb's plans sounded great but tended to veer dramatically in different directions once they got started.

"Wild hogs."

"Are you crazy?" Leesie squealed. "Those things will cut you to pieces."

"Nah, not the way we'll do it. My cousin built some hog traps. Once the hog is inside you can shoot it and drag it where you want."

"Your daddy ain't gonna let you go off by

yourself with a gun. If he will, your momma won't. Not that I blame her."

"Daddy said I could when I was thirteen."

"Yeah, but you're only eleven," she pointed out.

"Well, we could trap them then get my daddy or Mr. Robinson to go and shoot them. I'm sure they would. We'd need help dragging and cleaning them anyway."

"How we gonna make money off of hogs?" Johnny asked.

"Mr. Louis Cook is building a big smokehouse and he's going to make bacon and hams to sell to the city folks. I heard him tell Mr. Jenkins he could use all the hogs he could get."

"Did you ask him if he'd buy them?"

"Not exactly."

"What do you mean, 'not exactly'?"

"Well...no."

"Why on earth not?"

"What is Mr. Cook going to do if I ask him before I have the hogs?"

Leesie and Johnny both started to answer, but were interrupted by Caleb.

"That's right. He'd say something to my daddy or momma and then I'd have to explain what we were doing and why, how it wouldn't interfere with school or chores, how it's not dangerous, and so on and so on. It's easier to ask after I, I mean *we*, have the first hog trapped and just need help with the easy part." He gave an extra yank on Bo's tail to emphasize the brilliance of his reasoning. Bo snatched his head around, slinging slobber on Johnny, who grimaced and wiped it off.

"I don't know..." Leesie said.

"Do *you* have any other ideas on how to get money for Johnny's new mule?"

"No."

"Then it's settled," Caleb said with finality.

Leesie had a bad feeling, but then Caleb's schemes usually left her with a bad feeling and most of

65

them turned out all right. Well … kind of all right.

It took them three days of scrounging to gather enough materials for half a dozen traps, then another week, working after school and on the weekend, to drag it all down to the bottoms and build the traps. The final step was putting the traps where they wanted them and baiting them with some dried corn on the cob he'd snatched from the barn behind his house. They found out how good the traps worked when Johnny tripped one while baiting it and they spent a half hour figuring out how to release him.

"If it'll catch a boy, it'll catch a hog," Caleb proclaimed proudly.

They put the traps on paths the hogs used, easy to find because of the tracks and the hair and mud caught on trees where they'd scratch themselves. Every other day they'd go and check to see if they'd caught anything, as well as making side trips to keep an eye on the progress Mr. Cook was making on his smokehouse.

The traps yielded no hogs, but did catch a couple of squirrels, who were found happily munching on the corn until Bo appeared. The traps also managed to capture another of Mrs. Finstrom's cats and one of the camp dogs who growled at Bo when he was released, then ran off when Bo growled back.

"I just can't figure it," Caleb exclaimed. "The traps are good, the corn is good, I know there's hogs but they aren't going in the traps."

On their fifth trip to check the traps, it was obvious something was in the last one they checked. They could hear the trap shaking and the wood creaking as they approached.

"I told you it would work! I told you!" Caleb exclaimed, hopping up and down in excitement.

The cage shook as the hog threw itself back and forth. Bo ran around the cage barking loudly, causing the hog to shake the trap even more.

"Leesie, you run back and get Daddy and tell him to bring his gun and the mule," Caleb said. The hog threw itself against the cage again and Caleb heard a piece of wood crack. "And tell him to hurry!"

He grabbed Bo and wrestled him away from the trap, then, with Johnny's help, dragged him backwards until they were out of sight of the hog. Gradually the commotion dropped back to the original level.

"I reckon we'll make a pretty penny off of this one," Caleb said. "You gonna give all your money to your daddy?"

Johnny started nodding his head, then scrunched up his face and shook it instead.

"All except for enough to buy another soda pop for you, me, and Leesie. What you gonna do with your share?"

"I'm not gonna take a share. You and Leesie can split it."

"Why for?"

"Leesie's momma is always working so hard just to get by, and y'all need that mule. I've got Bo and I don't really need anything." He thought for a moment. "I'll tell you what though. Why don't we set aside enough to buy Leesie a new doll as a surprise? Hers is getting a little raggedy."

"That sho' sounds fine," Johnny said.

The noise from the cage started up again a few minutes later, interrupting the boy's conversation about their future riches. Bo started struggling and whining but with both Johnny and Caleb holding his collar they managed to keep him contained.

A huge crash sounded in the direction of the trap.

"Sounds like he broke it," Johnny said.

"I think he might've. Maybe we should go and take a look?"

"Maybe we should wait for your daddy."

Caleb thought for a second.

"No, I don't want him to come all the way down here to find out I couldn't build a good trap and wasted his time. I'm going to see what happened."

Caleb got to his feet and held Bo by the collar while he crept back to the location of the trap, Johnny reluctantly following along.

"Aw, he knocked the door loose," Caleb said as he got closer to the trap. "The pin slipped loose." He pointed to the pin dangling by a piece of string. "It must have been too small."

He picked up a stick and used his pocket knife to whittle a new pin that fit snugly.

"There, that'll do it," he said.

Johnny turned to leave.

"Where you going?" Caleb asked.

"Back to camp. Trap's empty now," Johnny pointed to the wooden and wire cage.

"Sure, but the hog is right in there," Caleb pointed to the thicket where a thrashing noise could be heard not far away. "I'm going to the other side of the bottom and chase him back this way into the trap again."

"You what?"

"I'm going to chase him into the trap. We'll put it right there where the path leads out of the thicket. He'll be running so fast he'll run right into it and we've got him again."

"You lost your mind. That hog's gonna eat you up."

"Naw, I'm just gonna throw rocks and stuff to make him think there's something coming after him. He'll run this way and back into the trap and we'll have him."

"Caleb, I don't think..." Johnny began, but Caleb interrupted him.

"It'll work fine. You just hold Bo."

Johnny took the hound by the collar as Caleb pushed the trap into position.

"You be careful," Johnny told him. "Don't let him get a'hold of you,"

"I'll be fine, you just listen and hold onto Bo."

Caleb and Johnny followed the edge of the

68

sawbriar thicket back around the hillside to the other side of the bottom. They stopped when the noise of the hog was directly between them and the trap.

Caleb reached down and picked up a large pine knot and flung it at the sound. A squeal indicated his aim had been right on. The noise moved in the direction of the trap.

Caleb scratched around with his foot until he found a rock and chunked it, but it fell short by several feet, as did a second rock and another pine knot.

"I'm gonna have to get closer," he said as he stuck a couple of rocks in his back pocket. He got onto his hands and knees and crawled into one of the tunnels the hogs had made through the briars.

"Caleb, I reckon that hog can run frontwards a lot faster than you can crawl backwards. Why don't we just wait for your daddy?"

"No, I ain't waiting. I'll just go in a little further and start throwing." Johnny no sooner saw the seat of Caleb's britches disappear around a bend in the tunnel than he saw them reappear even faster.

"Here he comes!" Caleb yelled. "Climb a tree!"

Johnny didn't have to be told twice. He let go of Bo and skinned up a small oak to the lowest branch, a good six feet off of the ground.

Caleb exploded backwards from the briars and jumped at a different tree, his feet making it to the lowest branch just as the big black hog erupted from the briar patch.

But they'd forgotten about Bo.

As the hog made it into the clear he was met by the teeth of the young dog, snapping at the hog from all directions as Bo whirled and danced around him.

This hog had had enough aggravation and, rather than retreating, chose to fight.

The fight seemed to last forever, but in reality it was only a minute or so. Bo was little more than an overgrown puppy, his adult teeth and jaw muscles not developed enough yet to do more than annoy the three hundred pound swine whereas the boar was a veteran of other dog fights as well as battles to maintain superiority in his herd.

The outcome of this fight was preordained.

With a quick flick of his tusks, the hog tried to disembowel the dog, which had been maneuvered into the tight space of hillside, trees and briars by the hog's efficient use of his bulk.

What the hog hadn't counted on was that Caleb's love for his dog would overcome whatever fear and common sense he should have had. As the hog prepared to do away with the dog, Caleb dropped from the tree and grabbed a thick limb from the ground, hitting the hog between the ears and distracting him long enough for Bo to bounce free from the tight space.

The hog turned his attention to the boy, ignoring the yapping dog biting at his flanks. Caleb tried to climb a pine tree, but the lowest limbs were out of reach and the bark stripped off of the trunk refusing to give his feet purchase.

The hog caught Caleb along the side of his leg, ripping through the denim of the pants and into the flesh beneath. The force of the blow threw the boy several feet to the side.

Quickly the hog followed up on his advantage, advancing on the boy lying prostrate on the ground and unable to get his leg to work and help him to his feet and the nearest tree.

Bo flashed in from the side, sinking his teeth into the only soft part of the pig he could reach, the ear. A loud squeal from the pig revealed that the dog had scored. The pig flipped his head back and forth, the dog swinging from him but refusing to release his grip.

The distraction gave Caleb time to make it to his feet, but the motion of doing so drew the attention of the boar again, and he charged in that direction, slowed slightly by the weight of the dog still clinging to his ear.

Caleb's leg was still too weak to allow him to climb, and he spun around to confront his attacker.

That was when Johnny entered the fracas.

Swallowing his fear, Johnny leapt from his perch and grabbed the hog by the curly tail when the beast was only a few feet away from Caleb. He hauled backwards with all of his strength, slowing the behemoth even more and allowing Caleb the chance to dodge behind a tree and grab a limb from the ground.

At that moment, Bo's grip on the ear succeeded in breaking through the tough cartilage, shredding the ear into ribbons. The dog wasted no time and jumped forward to slash at the snout of the pig, then darted away again.

The fight was rapidly leaving the hog, and just as he turned his attention to Johnny a gunshot boomed across the forest and with a lunge the pig broke free from Johnny's grip and ran into the woods. Bo followed for a short distance then returned to Caleb, who had fallen, ashen faced, to the ground.

"Did we get him?" he asked his father, who ran up holding the shotgun he had brought with him, Leesie at his side.

"No, he got away," his daddy said, taking his shirt off and wrapping it around the boy's bleeding leg.

"Is Bo okay?"

"He's fine."

"He's a good dog isn't he?" Caleb asked drowsily, his eyes fluttering.

"A fine dog."

"Johnny?" Caleb motioned for his friend.

"Yeah, Caleb?

"Thanks."

"You welcome."

Caleb slipped away into unconsciousness as his daddy handed the shotgun to Johnny and picked his son up to carry him back to camp.

CHAPTER 11

Picking Huckleberries

Every summer in central Louisiana, the branches of a scraggly, low to the ground, almost leafless bush suddenly burst forth with a sweet bounty, the huckleberry.

A wild cousin of the blueberry, similar in taste, a huckleberry is about the size of a buckshot and intensely sweet. Prized for the cobblers and jams that can be made from it, the scarcity of the bushes and the work required to gather them make the berries a prize often sought, but almost never obtained to the degree desired.

Caleb's leg had healed up and, despite an occasional twinge, was pronounced nearly as good as new, although it did leave him with a slightly noticeable limp. The fiasco with the hog and Johnny's willingness to risk himself to save Caleb made the boy even more determined than ever to help Johnny raise money.

"I've got another idea to raise some money" he announced one day as they were sitting around.

"No, no, no, Caleb Gandy!" Leesie said. "No more of your ideas."

"This one you'll like, I promise," he replied. "We'll pick huckleberries. Everybody in camp would want some and I bet Mr. Jenkins would buy all we could get."

"That does sound like a good idea," Leesie said. "Plus we could save some for ourselves."

"How much do huckleberries sell for?" Johnny asked.

"At least a quarter a bucket. Two hundred

buckets would pay for the mule. It'll be a lot of work, but we can have fun while we're doing it."

"Do you know where to find that many?"

"I know where there's some and I bet Ukiah knows where there are lots."

They rounded up six buckets from around camp and made their way up the hill to Ukiah's shack, where they found him sitting on his porch, sipping from a jar of moonshine and rocking, staring at his bottle tree.

"Howdy kids," he said as they walked up.

They returned his greeting.

"What'cha doing?" Caleb asked.

"Just studying the tree. Wondering if I caught any spirits yet."

"Do you think you have?" Johnny asked, eyes big at the thought.

"Mayhaps so. I expect if anything bad happened to Miss Callie she's right there in the red bottle, just waiting."

Caleb and Leesie went to look at the bottle, but Johnny hung back.

"I don't want nothin' to do with no spirits," he said. "Even Miss Callie's."

"I understand, but you've got to remember the spirits in the red bottle are good ones, just waiting for their mortal remains to be found and buried or for a friendly spirit to come along and lead them to heaven. Ain't no bad spirits here."

Johnny wrinkled up his face.

"I'll think about it."

"What are the buckets for?" Ukiah asked when Caleb and Leesie came back to the porch.

"Huckleberries. We're gonna pick 'em to sell and help Johnny's pa buy a mule."

"Oooo. I love huckleberries. I tell you what, I'll buy the first two buckets from you."

"It's a deal. Do you know of any good bushes?"

Ukiah leaned back in his chair and stroked his whiskers, deep in thought.

"Now that you mention it," he said eventually. "There used to be a patch with lots of them on the ridge above Murrell's Cave. Not many people go there because it's so steep, but I imagine you can find all the berries you want there. There's another place not too far from here, just off the creek that should be pretty good too. Might be a good place to start."

Ukiah squatted in the dirt, using a stick to draw them a map of how to get there. He'd occasionally push Bo out of the way, and redraw any parts the dog had messed up. Queenie just lay on the porch looking at her pup, only moving when Bo grabbed at the bone she had trapped under one paw, and then only to raise up and growl at him before laying back down.

The kids decided to try the closer spot first, and after a few wrong turns and twists, found the patch Ukiah had described. The first few handfuls went in their mouths, even Bo getting a taste before plunging into the creek for a cooling swim.

However, the *idea* of picking hundreds of buckets of huckleberries proved to be much more appealing than the *reality*, and soon the kids were covered in scratches from reaching in amongst the branches for the tiny berries. It seemed that no matter how long they picked, the buckets didn't get any fuller.

A few swimming breaks and several hours later the first six buckets were finally full and the bushes were picked clean except for the green berries which promised another crop in a week or two.

"Gosh, these are heavy." Leesie said as they started back to camp, with a stop at Ukiah's on the way to deliver his two buckets.

"They sure are," Johnny said, keeping a careful eye for snakes while trying not to spill any of the hard won berries.

"Dang it Bo!" Caleb yelled. "Stay out from under my feet!" Bo's enthusiasm for his boy made the job much more difficult.

Occasionally a spill would result from their

74

travels, and time would be spent searching for the elusive berries on the leaf and pine straw covered ground.

The first two buckets were delivered to Ukiah, Johnny and Leesie waiting at the bottom of the hill with the other four while Johnny trudged his way to the top.

The kids had agreed amongst themselves to give the two buckets to Ukiah for free, but the old man insisted on paying for them and handed Caleb a shiny, silver dollar.

"But that's more than we're charging anyway!" Caleb had protested.

"As much work as it takes to fill two buckets? They're cheap at that price. Besides, it'll help the Robinsons and they're good people." Caleb gratefully accepted the money when viewed in that light.

The other four buckets were sold shortly after entering camp, the first four houses they called on each buying a bucket.

"I love huckleberries," Mrs. Johnson said. "I'll holler at y'all when I make a cobbler."

It was obvious that hauling the buckets into camp a few at a time would take forever, but they were encouraged that they'd made two dollars in a day. That was more than most grown ups made.

Johnny had an idea.

"I bet daddy would let us use the mule," he volunteered. "He's not in good enough shape to plow, but he'd likely be okay for us to ride and to haul buckets of berries."

Johnny said he'd ask his daddy that night.

****

Early the next morning Caleb was awakened by a loud "hee haw" outside his yard.

"Got him huh?" he asked Johnny, who was perched proudly on top of the animal. Tied behind him were four wicker baskets, some empty syrup buckets, and a stack of old flour sacks.

"Daddy said it was fine and wanted me to thank you for helping us raise the money," Johnny said as he hopped off the mule. He reached into the pocket of his overalls and retrieved a silver dollar, holding it out to Caleb. "But he said that we had to split the money. It wouldn't be fair for us to keep it all."

Caleb thought for a moment.

"Well, that dollar will buy the doll for Leesie, with a little left over for soda pop. What's your daddy gonna do with this mule when he gets the new one?"

"Sell it I 'spect. But I'm not sure who would want a mule that can't plow."

"I would," Caleb said.

"You would?" Johnny asked. "What fo'?"

"I'm going to start coon hunting with Bo soon and I'll need a mule to keep up. Do you reckon your daddy would sell this one to me when he gets the new one? I don't have a place to keep him so he'd have to stay with you."

"I'm sure he would. That's just what we'll do."

"It's a deal then. You keep my share of the money and apply it to the mule and his upkeep. Leesie can have hers and everybody is happy. Going after the huckleberries will be a good way to test him out, see how he handles the hills and make sure he's not scared of Bo."

Since the dog was contentedly gnawing on the lower leg of the mule, who occasionally stomped his hoof to shake him off but otherwise ignored him, it didn't appear the dog-mule relationship would pose a problem.

The boys rode to Mr. Jenkins's store, bought the new doll for Leesie and got an agreement to pay a quarter for every bucket they brought him, then they rode to Leesie's.

"Here Johnny," Caleb said, handing the package wrapped in brown paper to him. "You give it to her."

Leesie started crying as she tore the paper open.

To Caleb's surprise, so did Johnny.

"What's the matter with you?" he asked.

"I ain't never give nobody a sho' nuff present before," Johnny said. "Just stuff I made."

Leesie squealed with delight when she saw the doll, flinging her arms first around Johnny, then Caleb, and planting a big kiss on each boy's cheek.

"She's beautiful!" the girl exclaimed.

"All right, that's enough mushy stuff," Caleb said in embarrassment. "We've got work to do."

"Can I bring her with me?" Leesie asked.

"She's yours, do what you want but her hair might get full of stickers and she'll probably smell like mule before the day's over."

Leesie thought for a moment, then carefully set the doll in the rocking chair on the front porch.

"You're right. I'll play with her when we get back." Leesie kept her head turned watching the doll until the mule turned the bend and the woods blocked it from her sight.

Caleb quickly learned that trails which were suitable for walking had to be reevaluated when riding a mule. In addition to the trail being too narrow in places, scraping their legs up against trees, he now had to contend with a third dimension, height. On the trail Ukiah had laid out the kids had to climb off the mule several times to get around trees and under tree limbs.

A lot of the trail was up and down sandy hillsides covered in pine straw and the mule had trouble handling the slippery terrain. The kids agreed they would find another route back to camp.

Upon arrival at the berry patch, they knew the trouble had been worth it. The hilltop was covered in bushes, each one loaded with the shiny blue huckleberries.

They quickly filled the wicker baskets and the pails, using the empty flour sacks as covers to keep any berries from bouncing out on the ride back home.

Even though there was nowhere near two

hundred buckets, they were still proud to know they were making a substantial contribution to Mr. Robinson's mule fund, plus they were getting to socialize. As an extra bonus they were getting to eat their fill of the berries without it interfering with them having enough to sell, and the bushes still had enough berries for one or two more trips.

Before heading back home they took a break to eat their lunch of fried ham and cornbread Mrs. Gandy had packed for them as well as drinking water from the "gen-u-wine" army canteen Caleb had gotten for Christmas last year. Of course, Bo joined in the feast and even the mule got a piece of cornbread and some water for his efforts.

The route home would have to be winding to avoid the branches and sandy hillsides, which meant braving the thickets and briars of the bottoms. Riding the mule meant fewer scratches though and Bo had an abundance of rabbits to chase, even though Caleb kept calling him off of them. It was widely agreed that chasing rabbits was a sure fire way to ruin a good coon dog.

"This load ought to make a pretty good dent in the mule fund, won't it Johnny?"

"I 'spect it will. I never realized white folks had so many ways they could make money."

"Being white ain't got nothing to do with it. Selling huckleberries ain't no different than selling vegetables, 'cept it's less work 'cause you ain't got to plow and plant and hoe, just pick. Daddy always says it's better to work smart than to work hard."

"He's sho' right."

The mule was walking through a clearing just then, huge brush piles, left over from the logging operation which had created the clearing, piled all around.

"You sure you know where we are?" Leesie asked Caleb.

"Yup. The creek's on our left a ways. If'n we

just keep going for a mile or so we'll hit one of the mule trails and it'll take us right into camp."

"You ever been here before?"

"Nope, but as long as we don't cross the creek or go back up a hill we have to come out okay."

Johnny started sniffing just as Bo's head popped up and he took off at a trot toward one of the larger brush piles.

"What's that smell?" Johnny asked.

"No Bo!" Leesie yelled. "He's after another skunk."

"That ain't no skunk," Caleb said. "You two wait up here."

He hopped off the mule and followed Bo, noticing that the ground was torn up where the wild hogs had been rooting around.

Bo's wiggling rear end could be seen sticking out of a pile of brush. He was shaking his head, worrying something in the pile. Just as Caleb approached he heard a ripping sound and Bo tumbled backwards, something clenched in his teeth.

"What'cha got boy?

Bo decided that what Caleb really wanted was a game of chase and took off running, something white fluttering from his jaws.

The smell had gotten stronger the closer Caleb had gotten to the brush pile. As he leaned over to peer inside it was so strong he gagged, and was about to abandon the effort when a flash of white buried in the branches caught his eye.

It took a moment, but he realized what he was looking at and stumbled backwards, trying hard not to vomit but failing.

"Caleb? What's wrong?" Leesie asked as she ran up, Johnny on her heels.

"Stay back," Caleb gasped, wiping his mouth on his shirt sleeve.

"What's that?" Johnny asked, peering into the brush pile.

79

"Miss Callie," Caleb said. "Or at least, what's left of her."

He vomited again.

CHAPTER 12

A Grisly Discovery

Every man in camp volunteered to search the area for clues, but many learned there is a dramatic difference between a good intention and a good deed once they got to the clearing. Several good men excused themselves and returned to camp after their initial view and smell of the area.

Most people don't realize that hogs, particularly wild ones, are omnivores, eating meat and plants with equal gusto. While the brush pile had protected much of Miss Callie's body, the hogs, along with every scavenger in the forest, had been at the exposed parts. Add to the bloated and torn body of the once beautiful woman a generous frosting of writhing maggots and the disbursal of several parts of the body around the clearing and even a man with a strong stomach had problems.

The sheriff was at the camp a few hours after they'd called and he, along with Caleb, led the procession to the clearing, the smell telling them they were in the right place. The boy, despite his protests, was made to wait a distance away, the fact that he'd already seen the worst making no difference to the adults.

Although the men combed the clearing and tore the brush piles to the ground, rags sprinkled with turpentine tied around their noses and mouths to help block the smell, no new evidence was found in the search. Some of the men were assigned to handling the remains and the rest spread out and followed what appeared to be a trail back toward camp, looking along the way for any clues as to what may have happened.

Mr. Gandy returned home after dark and went straight to the back porch and stripped before walking to the creek behind the house and washing with the strong, homemade lye soap. He scrubbed until his skin was raw and glowing red in the light from the kerosene lamp that Caleb held for him, but he didn't seem satisfied that he'd washed off the smell from the clearing.

Finally he walked back to the house covered only by the darkness of the night and handed the clothes he'd been wearing to Caleb.

"Burn them tomorrow," he said simply.

Caleb took the clothes to the burn pile and left them. When he returned to the house his daddy was sitting at the kitchen table, sipping whiskey from one of Ukiah's fruit jars.

"I hope I never have to do anything like that again," he said, taking another sip of the whiskey and waving his hand at the plate of food his wife put in front of him.

"You need to eat," she said.

"Not hardly," he replied, shaking his head.

"Caleb, maybe you ought to go to bed," his momma said to him.

"No honey, let him stay. He saw the worst and he's growing up. He handled it better than most of the men did."

His mother pursed her lips but didn't say anything else.

"Her throat was cut," Mr. Gandy said after a while. "The sheriff said he didn't know what else had been done, but her throat was cut."

"Oh, George. That poor woman."

"We're going to have a service for her tomorrow. You make sure all of the women in camp are at the funeral."

"I will."

"I know y'all didn't approve of her, but the least

82

we can do is show her the respect of coming to the service. Because of her...condition...we buried her in the cemetery tonight and spoke a few words over her, so there won't be a coffin, but we'll still have the service."

"I'm sure everybody in camp will be there."

"We're shutting down work tomorrow, so there won't be any excuses for anyone to miss. I'll be more than a little upset if any of the 'gentlemen' who used to visit her are too embarrassed to show up now. Including the married ones."

"Does the sheriff have any idea who might have...you know?"

"None. The only clue may be that Dan Jenkins swears the dress she was wearing was the same one she had on when she was at the store the last time she was seen. Did you ever know Callie to wear the same dress two days in a row?"

"Her? Absolutely not. That's one of the reasons a lot of women didn't care for her. They've only got two dresses and Callie had more than a dozen. So what happens now?"

"You mean after the service? I expect the sheriff will poke around and ask questions but unless something really unusual happens it won't amount to spit. Whoever did it will likely get away with it and we'll never know who did it or why."

"But it had to be someone we know."

"There weren't any strangers passing through, just camp folks so you're probably right."

"It just doesn't seem possible that someone here could do something like that."

"They did though."

"Daddy?"

"Yes Caleb?

"Is someone going to get in touch with her parents and daughter?"

"I imagine the sheriff will. I'll likely write them a letter of sympathy from the folks here in camp. Not

83

sure what I'll say, but something will come to me."

"Did you find her watch?"

"What watch?"

"She carried a pocket watch her husband had given her. She showed it to us when we were over there the last time. It was silver. If you find it I think her daughter would like to have it."

"No, there wasn't any watch but it could still be in the house, the clearing, or anywhere between here and there."

"Miss Callie was nice," the boy said.

"We all have our faults, but you are right. Callie was a nice person."

"I'll miss her."

CHAPTER 13

Johnny Goes to School

School was out for the summer, which meant plenty of time for fishing and swimming, games of cowboys and Indians, marbles, fights and reconciliations, all, of course, after chores were completed.

Caleb had a summer of fun planned. Rumor at his house was that there would be a visit to the big city of Natchitoches sometime with a trip to a sure enough movie theater. His chores were minimal and could be completed in an hour or less, particularly if neither parent took the time to inspect the quality of his work.

He planned for fishing to eat up a major portion of his time, thanks to a new rod and reel he'd gotten for his birthday. So far most of the time he'd spent with it involved untangling the line from either trees or the inevitable "bird's nest" that resulted from the line tangling on itself on the spool. He was determined to have it mastered by the time school started back.

However, his main project for the summer involved Bo. Coon hunting would occupy most of his nights. His father had finally agreed that if Caleb earned the money himself he could buy a .22 rifle of his own. He figured that the raccoons he and Bo could catch over the summer would go a long way toward the purchase, selling the skins and the meat. In the meantime he'd borrow his dad's rifle, although he was still responsible for the ammunition.

On the first day of summer vacation Caleb woke early, grabbed his rod and reel, and stuffed a couple of biscuits wrapped in a napkin in his pocket.

"Come on Bo," he said, the dog jumping to his feet and following him out the door.

Caleb whistled as he strode toward Leesie's house, happy to have three months of carefree fun in his future. He opened the gate to Leesie's yard and stepped in, careful to nudge a chicken out of the way so it wouldn't escape through the gate while it was open.

His whistling ended abruptly when he looked around the yard.

In the shade of a big oak tree, Leesie stood behind a small table. She was wearing her best dress, threadbare though it was. On the table were an apple, chalk, and three slates like they used in school.

In front of the table were three chairs, facing her. Johnny sat in one of the chairs, her new doll was in another, and the third was empty. Johnny turned when he heard Caleb and smiled widely.

"You're late," Leesie said.

"No, no, NO!" Caleb exclaimed. "It's summertime! No school during summertime! It's a law or something. Do you want us to get arrested?"

"Stop being silly. We told Johnny I'd teach him to read and write."

"I didn't say I would! Why don't you wait for school to start back up?"

"Because we don't have time after school with all the work Johnny has to do. Now hush up and sit down. We'll only do it for a little while at a time and then we can do something else."

"Why do I have to sit down? I already know how to read and write."

Leesie pinched his arm and said in a whisper loud enough for him to hear but not loud enough to carry to Johnny, "Hush! Do you want to hurt his feelings? Now sit down."

Caleb flopped onto the vacant chair and pouted for the entire session. He'd occasionally sneak a bite of his biscuit, or pass a bite to Bo, until Leesie caught him and scolded him just like they were in real school.

Johnny caught on fast and by the time the school was over he could recite the alphabet through L, read and write through E, and do addition and subtraction on the numbers 1 through 5.

"You sho' are a good teacher, Lees...Miss Leesie," Johnny said.

Early in the session she had rapped Caleb across the knuckles with her "ruler", really just a stick, and instructed them both to call her Miss Leesie when school was in session.

Despite Caleb's commands, Bo had refused to bite Leesie, instead just yawning and thumping his tail on the ground, not even deigning to rise from his prone position.

Leesie disappeared into the house and returned with two small plates and cups from her tea set and giving one of each to the boys. The plates had fresh cookies and the teacups contained cold milk.

"This is for being such good students," she said.

Unfortunately, several of the boys from camp chose that moment to walk by the "school yard".

"Aw, isn't that sweet? Caleb and Leesie are having a tea party," one of the boys said.

"Where are your dollies, Caleb?" another one yelled.

When Caleb didn't respond, the boys took it as a sign of weakness and the catcalls increased, broken only by the discovery that Caleb's silence was less an indication of indifference and more a result of his concentration on locating the perfect collection of rocks. This misperception on the part of the boys was quickly remedied when the first stones struck their targets and the boys beat a hasty retreat, discretion being the better part of valor. Two of the boys were forever shamed, first because they cried after being struck by the rocks and second, because the crying was prompted by projectiles launched from Leesie's hand.

Johnny, well aware of the color issue, abstained from taking part. The decision was easier since Caleb and Leesie didn't need any help.

"How long are we going to have to do this?" Caleb asked after he had finished his snack.

"Eat?"

"Ha ha. No, I mean school. How long are you going to make us go to school?"

"I'm not making *y'all* go to school. Johnny wants to go. *You're* the only one who's a problem. Even Bo likes it here."

"That's because you keep feeding him cookies."

Leesie stuck her tongue out at him and rapped her knuckle busting stick on the table.

"Class is dismissed. Y'all wait while I change into my play clothes." She ran to the house carrying the empty plates and cups, then paused on the front porch to shout back over her shoulder. "School is at the same time tomorrow. I expect you both to be here."

"Yas'sum," said Johnny, the smile back in place.

Caleb just grunted and nudged Bo with the toe of his shoe.

"Why didn't you bite her?"

To Caleb, it looked like Bo laughed at him before he laid his head back down in the dirt to resume his nap.

"Y'all want to come fishing with me?" Caleb asked when Leesie emerged in her play clothes.

Both of them nodded their assent, so the trio returned to Caleb's house to retrieve two cane poles and dig for a few more worms.

"Quiet now," Caleb whispered as he gently removed the shovel from under the porch. "If momma sees me with this shovel in my hand it'll remind her that the winter garden needs the ground turned and fertilized and that'll take three or four days, plus another couple of days for the stink to wash off."

The garden was fertilized with the manure gathered from the chicken coops which almost every family had behind their house. The manure was so rich it had to be carefully laid out and turned with the dirt to allow slow decomposition, killing weeds at the same time that it nourished the soil. By wintertime the garden would be ready to burst forth with potatoes, cabbages, carrots, and other cold weather crops.

"I'll help you, if you'll help me," Johnny said, looking at Caleb and feigning a lack of concern.

"I don't like you that much," Caleb said with a smile. Caleb's garden was small, barely big enough to provide food for the family. Johnny, however, lived on the edge of gardens which were acres in size and required wagon loads of the smelly, slimy manure. Turning it under was easy with a mule and plow, but the boy's job was to stand in the back of the wagon being driven by Johnny's mother and throw the manure behind it a shovelful at a time while his daddy walked behind with the plow.

They were almost clear of the house when Caleb heard the door slam behind him and his mother's voice yelled out, "Caleb! You get back here!"

He hunched his shoulders as the voice rang out, weighed the possibility of avoiding her by pretending he didn't hear (unlikely) then turned and slunk back to his house, the shovel dragging in the dirt behind him.

Leesie, Johnny, and Bo followed him.

"Yes'm?" he said as he reached the porch.

"What were you fixin' to do?"

"Go fishing. Well, dig some worms and then go fishing."

"Put that shovel up."

Caleb's face brightened slightly as he chunked the shovel under the porch. She wouldn't have had him do that if chicken manure was in his immediate future.

"Mr. Cook stopped by a few minutes ago looking for you."

That was curious. Louis Cook worked at the turpentine mill, and had started the smokehouse business, but was best known for his hunting and fishing abilities.

"You haven't been up to any mischief have you?"

Caleb quickly searched his memory, then ran the query through his mind in case it was a trick question, the kind parents sometimes used to trap a kid into denying something they already knew full well he had done.

"No ma'am?" He didn't remember doing anything likely to cause him parental grief, but wasn't sure enough to declare it emphatically.

"He wants you three to come up to his house and visit him. Said he had something to show you. Mind your manners now, you hear?"

"Yes'm," the three said, and turned to leave.

"You may as well leave your fishing poles here. When you get finished at Mr. Cook's you come on back here and get to work on the winter garden."

"Yes'm," he said, shoulders slumping in dejection as he walked. "Never," he mumbled to himself, "never hesitate when work is waiting on you."

"You mean you should have went ahead and done the garden and got it out of the way?" Leesie asked.

"No," Johnny replied. "I mean I should have kept moving when I heard Momma's voice."

****

Mr. Cook's house was a little way off from the camp, and as they approached they could hear the barking of a bunch of dogs. Caleb took a piece of rope from his back pocket and used it as a leash for Bo.

A man in a pair of overalls and a short sleeved shirt was washing blood from his hands with the water pouring from a pump spout. He'd pump for a few moments, then rub his hands forcefully under the flow with a piece of soap until the water stopped, at which time he'd pump again.

"Howdy Mr. Cook," Caleb said as he walked

90

up. Bo was straining against the rope, trying to get to one side of the yard where an assortment of dogs were tied. Several were obviously coonhounds, but most were amalgamations of different breeds, selected for their hunting abilities rather than their pedigrees or looks.

"Hi Caleb, Leesie. Good morning Johnny."

Mr. Cook knew Johnny through his daddy and occasionally bought vegetables from him on his deliveries to camp.

"Bo sure is looking good. Have you started training him yet?" he continued.

"A little bit. Now that it's summer time I should be able to work with him more."

"You gonna enter him in the contest this year?"

"I expect so."

Every summer the coon hunters in the area got together to show off their dogs. There were prizes for the most barks per minute on a treed coon, the fastest dog, the best nose, and many others. The dog with the most points at the end of the day got a blue ribbon and the owner got a cash prize. While the money would be nice, the blue ribbon and the bragging rights that went with it were just as important to Caleb.

"He'll do fine, although he's up against some stiff competition. I hear Lynn Bates is going to bring that big ol' Redbone hound of his this year. You know he won the whole shooting match three years in a row so they made him lay out for a couple of years and give some other people a chance."

"Yes sir. That is a fine hound but he's getting a little long in the tooth so Bo may have a surprise or two for him. No matter what, he's in for a fight."

"I imagine you're right."

Mr. Cook filled five buckets with water from the pump.

"Would y'all each grab one of these? I've got something you're going to be interested in."

The three kids followed behind Mr. Cook as he

made his way around the corner of the house.

In the back yard a cast iron cauldron big enough to take a bath in sat on top of a fire, steam rising off the water. To one side, on an A frame made of oak saplings hung a huge, black boar. Mr. Cook dumped his two buckets of water into the big pot, then did the same with the ones carried by the children.

"Is that..." Caleb started, then cut himself off with a big gulp.

"Sure is. Or at least I believe it is," he pointed to the hog's shredded ear. "He's got some tooth marks on his snout too. Didn't Bo get him there?"

"I don't really remember," Caleb said. "I was kind of busy."

"I remember," Johnny spoke up. "Bo got him on the nose and ear."

The boy squatted and looked at the curly tail of the boar.

"That's the same hog."

"Recognize him from that angle?" Caleb asked Johnny, who quickly stood up.

"Same hog," he repeated.

"How'd you get him?" Caleb asked.

"I had the dogs down in the bottom where you found him. They started causing a ruckus and he came shooting out of the briars. He surprised me so much I missed him with the first shot."

He pointed at a bullet hole just behind and slightly below the ear.

"But I got him with the second one. I had to get the mule to haul him here."

The hog's head hung a good foot above Mr. Cook's and his rear feet dragged the ground.

"He's bigger than I remember," Caleb said.

"Not me. I thought he was twice that big." This came from Johnny

And you jumped on him anyway, Caleb thought to himself. A good thing for me that you did.

"What's the hot water for?" Leesie asked.

"When you clean a hog you got to scrape the bristles off first," Mr. Cook replied. "Just like your daddy uses hot water when he shaves, I'm gonna use hot water to loosen the bristles up."

"Will he be good eatin'?" Caleb asked.

"Fair to middlin'," Mr. Cook replied. "Boars have a strong, wild flavor but if you cure it just right and smoke it long enough the bacon and hams will be good. The rest of the meat can be used to season beans and such. I'll be sure and save a ham and a side of bacon for y'all to share. You certainly earned it, especially you Johnny. Did you really jump out of a tree and grab him by the tail?"

Johnny shrugged and looked uncomfortable at having attention focused on him.

"He sure did," Caleb said. "Bravest thing I ever saw."

"Bravest or most foolish, I ain't sure which. Whatever possessed you to do such a thing? What were you thinking?"

"I wasn't really thinkin'. I didn't want Caleb or Bo to get eat up and it's the only thing that popped into my mind."

"Well, that answers the question. I agree with you Caleb, it was the bravest thing I've ever even heard of." Mr. Gandy pointed his knife toward the right rear leg of the hog. "I'm going to save that ham right there for you Johnny. I'd consider it an honor if you'd let me deliver it right to your door."

"Thank you Mr. Cook. We ain't never had no whole ham before."

"People who take care of their friends should be rewarded," Mr. Cook said. "What do you kids have planned for today?"

"We were going fishing in the creek, but Momma said I've got to fertilize and turn the garden," Caleb said.

"That reminds me," Mr. Cook said, stopping his work on the hog to look at the kids. "Y'all be extra careful down along the creek. I'm starting to set out my trap lines now and I've got them scattered all over so the man smell has time to wear off. Once they're set y'all mind you don't get caught in them. They won't take a foot off but they'd sure hook you up for a while and might even break a bone or two. You may want to teach Bo to stay away too. Every year I have to get a trap off of somebody's dog that got tangled up. Be especially careful of the big one set down by the otter slide. It'd definitely hurt you if it gets a'hold of you."

"We'll keep an eye out," Caleb said. The other two nodded in assent.

They made small talk for a few more minutes then excused themselves to head back to Caleb's house.

"The only thing worse than fertilizing the garden is fertilizing the garden when it's hot," Caleb observed.

When they got back to the house he told them good-bye, but they surprised him by remaining, Leesie grabbing another shovel and Johnny handling the wheelbarrow.

"I was just kidding about you having to help with our garden," Johnny said. "I'll help you anyways." Caleb silently committed to himself that any time Johnny had to work fertilizing the big garden, he'd be right there next to him. Leesie's garden was so small it wouldn't take an hour, so they decided to do it as soon as they finished his.

"Does this make me a teacher's cat?" Johnny asked when they'd finished with Leesie's winter vegetable patch.

"Pet, Johnny. A teacher's pet." She shot a look at Caleb to stop his laughing. "And yes it does."

"Oh brother," Caleb moaned.

CHAPTER 14

Fourth of July

The Fourth of July was always a big deal at the camp. The Company sprang for pigs to roast, hams and turkeys, and all of the families brought their best dishes to share.

Long tables were constructed out of freshly sawn planks and set up in front of the church. To one side the pigs were roasted on a spit above a firepit full of hickory wood, cut and set aside to dry months ago just for this occasion. The hams had been hanging in smokehouses for weeks, slowly absorbing the flavor and curing, ready now to be sliced and served.

Chicken and dumplings, cornbread dressing, pickled and fresh vegetables, biscuits and cornbread rounded out the main courses, with other tables covered with vegetables, cakes and pies of every description. A wagon full of watermelons bought by the Company from the Robinsons had been hauled in by their new mule, Abraham.

"I sure do appreciate this," Mr. Robinson had told Caleb's dad as he counted out the money for the watermelons at the building that served as the company office. "We was slowly getting the money together for the mule, but this put us over the top."

"It's a good deal for both of us," Mr. Gandy had responded. "Latham wanted twice as much to go to Natchitoches and pick up a load. Mind you watch out for him. I expect he'll be more than a little upset that he's going to be short on whiskey money."

Latham was vocal about "the company favoring a nigger over a white man" although the loss of business didn't appear to affect his ability to buy liquor since he was drunk well before the meal was served at noon.

Ukiah had even come down from his hill to partake in the festivities, contributing gallons of syrup to put on the biscuits, baskets of corn on the cob and, carefully stashed away for use by the men after the fireworks that night, a case of his best corn liquor.

The kids played games all morning while the women worked to finish cooking and load the tables up. The men were careful to stay out of the way, sitting to one side while they chewed tobacco or smoked, occasionally being called on for some heavy lifting or to taste a dish and give their opinion.

There would be another meal right before dark, but it would be leftovers from the lunch meal and not as eagerly anticipated.

Some of the men competed in games after lunch, the potato sack race being popular as were the watermelon seed spitting contest and the turkey shoot, which was really a shooting contest involving paper targets.

Caleb's favorite was the pie eating contest. A kid really didn't have a chance to win, but it was always fun to compete. The fact that a lot of the pies would be made with the huckleberries purchased from them made it even better.

The Robinsons were one of several black families partaking that day. It was an unspoken rule that they ate last, but there was always so much food that they got fed just as good as everyone else. The sole exception to the rule was Johnny, who was ushered into line between Leesie and Caleb. A few of the people gave him peculiar looks, but no one said anything as he filled his plate and sat with Caleb and the other white boys to eat. If he would have been paying attention he would have noticed he was the only black face in the group, the other negro children keeping to themselves a distance away. Instead, the excitement of the day got the best of him and he laughed and played with the white children forgetting, for the day at least, that he was different in the most profound way he could have been different in that day and age.

He even managed to win the blue ribbon and a pocket knife in the foot race by easily outdistancing the competitors. Even with his limp Caleb took third place, but was as happy about Johnny winning as if he'd been the victor himself. It was the first time in camp history that a negro had been allowed to compete with white children, but few even noticed and even fewer mentioned it, Ed Latham being the notable exception.

Bo had as much fun as the kids, tussling with other dogs, steadily getting fed by Caleb, Leesie, and Johnny, and generally making a nuisance of himself, often approaching folks and pushing his head under their hands until they scratched him behind the ears. The dog had a way of ingratiating himself, even to people who didn't care for animals. The hound was definitely a camp favorite.

The hayride was a popular attraction as well, the younger kids using the time to throw hay at each other and horse around while the teen agers discreetly held hands and occasionally stole a kiss.

The most anxiously awaited events were the fireworks and the bonfire. Beginning in June the men took turns clearing a space at the edge of camp, removing all of the leaves and pine straw so the sparks didn't set any buildings or the woods on fire. Even so, the eight man firefighting pump was filled to the brim with creek water and placed next to the clearing, a crew of men assigned to stand by it in case of an accident. In a community built entirely of dried wood, situated in the middle of a pine forest, no chances would be taken with a possible fire.

The pyrotechnics went off without a hitch, the ooohs and aaahs of the crowd rewarding the man who had come all the way from Alexandria, 80 miles on rutted forest roads, to bring the fireworks to the camp.

The very few errant sparks were quickly extinguished by the men using wet burlap sacks and the pump was rolled close to the bonfire, just in case.

Attendance around the bonfire was as segregated as possible. No black families attended, even the Robinsons having chosen to make their way home after the fireworks. The men would gather on a set of log sections cut years ago for just this purpose. The women tended to stand, not wanting to dirty their dresses or appear unladylike by sitting on stumps or the ground. The children ran wild, but were careful not to disturb any of the adults lest they be called down and forced to sit with their parents or, even worse, taken home for the remainder of the festivities.

Ukiah's case of whiskey was finally opened, the jars of clear yet potent liquid passed among the men as they discussed camp business, fishing, the weather, and other important manly topics, occasionally getting up to stamp out wayward sparks or helping to take down the frames that had been used for the fireworks.

Of course, after the women left the conversation it turned to the biggest news that had ever hit the camp, the death of Callie Monroe.

The storekeeper, Mr. Jenkins, reveled in being the center of attention, an honor bestowed upon him as the last white person to see Miss Callie alive, as well as being the person who knew the most about her.

"How old was she?" one of the men asked.

"Thirty two. She was thirty two years old last January," Mr. Jenkins answered.

"How'd she end up here?"

"She was traveling with a man who showed up here asking for work a couple of years ago," Jenkins said. "He worked here about three months then the sheriff showed up one day, slapped the handcuffs on him and took him off. I heard they sent him to Angola Prison. Anyways, Callie just stayed on and did what she had to do to survive."

"She was sure pretty," a voice said from the

darkness.

"Nice too," another unseen man volunteered.

There was silence for a while as the jars of liquor were passed from man to man.

"Damn shame that something like that would happen to such a nice woman," another voice said after a while.

"You know what's a damn shame?" A man spoke, badly slurring his words. He took a few steps into the firelight, a container of whiskey firmly gripped in his hand. Ignoring long accepted protocol he maintained his grip on the jar, not passing it to the next man in line.

"What Ed?"

"It's a damn shame that everybody in this camp knows who's responsible, but nobody will do a damn thing about it," Ed Latham said, the fire glittering in his watery eyes.

"Who's responsible?" A new man asked.

"That pet coon of Gandy's, Luther Robinson."

"You don't know that, Ed," Jenkins said, but took a step back as Latham took one toward him.

"Damned if I don't! It doesn't take much to figure it out."

Ed began holding up fingers as he made his points.

"First, he was the last person to be seen with her. Second, it was just before dark on the day she disappeared. Third, it would take somebody strong to have hauled her body all that way and Luther Robinson is a big buck nigger. As soon as I heard he was slobbering around her trying to get in good by carrying her groceries I knowed it was him. Nothing good ever comes of black folks mixing with white ones."

"The way I remember it, Miss Callie asked Luther to help her," Mr. Jenkins said. "He was already there at the store waiting on me to fill his order when she came in."

Ed Latham lunged at Mr. Jenkins, grabbing him

99

by the shirt front before the storekeeper managed to jerk free from the drunken man's grip.

"You shut up!" Latham snarled at him. "You just want to stay on Gandy's good side, always kowtowing to him and his nigger. You know as well as I do that he's responsible."

He lunged at the storekeeper again, but Mr. Jenkins managed to stay out of his grasp as Latham staggered around the uneven ground.

"Maybe Ed has a point," one of the men said.

"You think Luther killed her?" another asked.

"I'm not saying that he did, but he sure seems like the most likely suspect. I'm just wondering why he isn't locked up until they clear him"

Mutters of assent began coming from the dark as the mood of the men began turning ugly.

"Exactly!" Latham said, excited to find a receptive audience, or at least one that was more receptive than usual. "He ought to at least be locked up while they investigate. None of the women are safe as long as he's walking free."

More grumbling from around the fire.

"I think it may be time to take matters into our own hands. We could grab that nigger and make him talk." The excitement in Latham's voice evidenced that he believed he was on the verge of accomplishing his goal.

"That's why you shouldn't think, Ed," a voice said from the dark.

Mr. Gandy and Ukiah stepped into the light from the fire.

"I don't remember you being elected sheriff."

"Look Gandy, we're tired of Robinson being coddled. The only reason he isn't locked up right now is because you're protecting him for some reason. His little pickaninny son is even spending more time with your boy than with the other nigger children."

"The reason he isn't locked up is because there isn't anything, other than your loud mouth, saying he should be. And who my son, and for that matter, the Robinson boy, chooses for a friend is none of your business. Right now I'd say Caleb does a better job of picking his friends than I do of hiring people, but that can be fixed pretty quickly."

Several of the men got his point and faded back into the dark, jobs being scarce and most of them not too caught up in acting against Luther Robinson anyway.

But Ed Latham was too drunk to know when to quit.

"What about our women? As long as he is walking around free they can't sleep nights."

"I hadn't noticed you having a woman here in camp, Ed. The way I hear it, you're the one who's heavy handed with the ladies."

"You son of a bitch!" Latham growled and dropped his hand to his knife, taking a step toward Mr. Gandy.

"I don't believe I'd do that," Ukiah said, speaking for the first time. The firelight danced off of the blade of a huge Bowie knife that had suddenly appeared in his hand.

"You're drunk, Ed," Mr. Gandy said. "And I'll assume that's why you're acting like this. Go home and sleep it off before we both do something we'll regret."

Ed Latham snarled something under his breath, but turned away and stumbled into the darkness, heading in the general direction of his house. His cursing and the noise of his passage gradually receded into the distance.

The men stood in silence for a while, the jugs of moonshine again being passed from hand to hand.

A few more turns of the jugs around the fire and Mr. Gandy spoke.

"You know, it's might easy for somebody to get a wild hair in their ass and then go off and do something stupid. Usually, it'd be hard to convince folks to join you but there's something about whiskey," as he said this he held up a jar and shook it, making it appear the fire was dancing inside of it, "that makes people do stupid stuff. Pretty soon a really bad idea takes hold and a bunch of grown men take off on some fool task and..."

He stopped talking, took a swig from the jug, and threw the rest into the bonfire, where it flared up suddenly, startling the men.

"... boom," he finished, then handed the jar back to Ukiah.

"Good whiskey," he said, then tipped his hat to the rest of the men. "Good night. I expect all of you at work bright and early in the morning. Happy Fourth of July."

He turned and walked into the dark.

CHAPTER 15

A Nighttime Visit

Several weeks passed and Ed Latham continued his grumbling, although he was careful not to do it when Mr. Gandy was around. Caleb's daddy knew about it, but had made up his mind to ignore it until Latham brought things to a head.

The last straw was when Ed, working his axe, dropped a tree toward Luther Robinson's crew. Only quick action on Luther's part prevented the loss of any of his men. When he heard a creak and turned to see the tree swaying he yanked a pin loose from the chain, allowing his load of logs to slide back down the hill and freeing the mule team. His shout of "Head's up!" allowed his crew to leap to safety. The mules didn't move fast enough and one of them was struck by a limb on the tree, killing it instantly.

Mr. Gandy was on the scene in minutes.

"What happened?"

Ed Latham jumped forward.

"Tree jumped and swung off track. The dumb nigger didn't hear me holler 'Timber' and walked his mules under it." He spat a stream of tobacco to punctuate his disgust and then looked around as if daring someone to contradict him.

"Is that what happened?" Mr. Gandy asked Luther.

"Naw suh."

"What happened?"

"He didn't yell nothing. I'd started up the hill with the crew and the next thing I knew I saw the tree falling."

Mr. Gandy walked over to the tree and examined the cut, then walked to the stump and inspected it, before returning to where the men from the various crews had congregated to try and cut the dead mule free from the one that was still alive and struggling against the harness which held him in place. He helped free the animal, then stroked the muzzle as he slowly chewed his tobacco, rolling it from side to side in his mouth.

Eventually the mule calmed down and Mr. Gandy turned to look at the men, bringing his attention to focus on Ed Latham.

"Ed," he said, pausing to expectorate a brown stream of juice at the stalk of a thistle plant next to the trail. "You're fired."

"You're taking this murdering nigger's side against mine?"

"Shut up Ed! I can smell the whiskey on you from here. I told you if you showed up for work one more time after you'd been drinking you were fired."

"I don't think you can fire me."

"If you mean I don't have the power, you're wrong. If you mean I don't have the strength, you're wrong about that too. Don't test me Ed. Don't let that alligator mouth overload your hummingbird ass."

He spat in emphasis.

One of the men reached over and took the axe from Ed's hands.

Ed turned to leave, then suddenly darted toward Luther, his right hand reaching toward back and whipping his knife from his scabbard.

The knife never reached it's target. Luther's whip cracked once, knocking the knife from Ed's hand and laying it open in a spray of blood.

Latham cried out and fell backwards as Luther gathered the whip back into coils in his hand.

"Help him up," Mr. Gandy said.

As two men helped Latham to his feet, a third took a blue bandana from his pocket and wrapped it

104

around the bleeding hand, stanching the flow of blood.

"I can't make you move out of your house Ed, at least not yet. But since you no longer work for the company your rent is now $50 a month, payable in advance on the first of every month. If it isn't paid by the second, you're out. Now go back to camp and get that hand looked at."

The wounded man stumbled toward camp, gradually disappearing from sight down the trail through the pine forest. At a nod from Mr. Gandy, one of the work crew followed behind.

"All right now, you men get back to work. Luther, y'all need to get that tree off'n the mule and then drag it off way down in the woods. Your crew is gonna be off log duty until we can get another team in here, or at least another mule to replace the dead one."

"Yas'suh," Luther replied. The black men on his crew began hacking at the tree without comment, although the looks on their faces betrayed their worry at being out of work even for a few days. Times were tough for the white workers, but for the negroes in the crews a few days without even their meager pay meant the children would go to bed with their stomachs growling from hunger.

"Y'all know I can't pay you when you're not working, but I'll talk to Mr. Jenkins over at the store and let him know to let you slide for a while on your accounts and I'll try to get some work for you at the camp in a day or two. Best I can do."

"Thank you suh," the men mumbled, slightly more at ease, but only slightly. The bills would still have to be paid, each man already calculating where he could earn a few extra dollars.

****

Lydia Boyd had only been in camp a few weeks. One of the workers had found her in the red light district of Shreveport and told her about the camp and the opportunities for a lady of a certain moral inclination.

So far the men at the camp had been very good to her, both in their treatment and financially. She'd managed to save about half of what she had earned.

On this night she was taking a break from business and using the time to straighten up the house and do her laundry. Her little dog ran in and out of her feet as she finished washing her meager dishes and prepared to gather the laundry off of the clothes line strung across her back porch. As she went to the bedroom to fetch her clothes basket the dog started yapping.

"Hush Toby," she said. Although the house, like the one Miss Callie had stayed in, was on the outskirts of the camp she knew the women would use any excuse to dislike her, even the barely heard barking of her little dog.

Despite her instructions Toby continued to make noise, now intermingling his barking with diminutive growls and scratching at the screen door leading to the back porch.

"What's got into you?" she asked as she nudged him out of the way with her foot, pushing the screen door open with her basket.

Her kerosene lamps cast a dim light outside but as she turned she saw a man standing just at the edge of the glow. In his gloved hands was a large knife that he moved back and forth, causing the blade to catch what little light the lamps gave off. His dark features and clothing blended into the shadow, only the whites of his eyes and the sparkle of the blade clearly visible.

Lydia screamed and took a step backward. The dog's barking becoming frantic as he sensed the danger to his mistress.

The man appeared startled at the scream and moved quickly toward the house.

Lydia was young in years, but had lived a hard life in the brothels, first in New Orleans and then in

106

Shreveport. No shrinking violet, she had been confronted with dangers before, once by a robber and several other times by drunken and violent patrons. She realized any hesitation or timidity could potentially be fatal so she acted quickly, throwing the empty wicker basket at the man, causing him to flinch.

She took advantage of his hesitation and reached up, grabbing the clothesline and yanking it down and across the steps to the porch, the clean sheets fluttering down slowly. She then wheeled about and flung the screen door open and ran through it and into the house, Toby taking the opportunity to run out past her and onto the porch.

Lydia slammed the wooden door to the back porch and twisted the key to lock it, still screaming for help. Before she turned to run to the front door she glanced quickly through the window into the back yard, just in time to see the man fall to the porch, tangled in the clothesline and sheets.

Toby was launching a vigorous but ineffective attack as she ran out the front door and leapt to the path to camp running as fast as she could for the protection of its inhabitants.

****

Caleb stood with the crowd of men as dawn broke around Lydia's cabin. He'd awoken during the night when men from the camp had come for his father, who'd grabbed a pistol from under the bed and joined them to look for the almost-assailant, to no avail. While the men had been searching, Mrs. Gandy had taken a distraught Lydia under her wing, fixing tea and calming her. Several other women appeared and began cooing over the previously ignored member of the camp.

His daddy had soon returned, unsuccessful in the search. He'd waited until near daylight, sent a man for the sheriff, then, along with many others, accompanied the woman back to her house so they

107

could recreate what happened before anything could be disturbed further.

"Where was he when you first saw him?" Mr. Gandy asked.

"Right about there," Lydia replied and pointed. "Right at the very edge of the light."

"Did you get a good look at his face? Could you identify him again if you saw him?"

"I don't believe so. I only saw him for a second. Coal black skin was all I can remember."

The men around Caleb started muttering. Off to one side Bo was rolling on the ground with Toby, the little dog darting in and out, playfully nipping at him.

Caleb's daddy poked at the tangle of sheets and clothesline with the toe of his boot, then knelt and untangled the knot and examined it closer. He held it up for the men to see several slashes in the sheets.

"I assume these weren't there before?"

"No sir," Lydia said. "He must have cut them when he got tangled and fell."

"What about this?" Mr. Gandy pointed to a black smudge on a sheet.

"The sheets were washed fresh before I hung them up. They were as white as snow."

Mr. Gandy rubbed the smudge between his fingers, then smelt them.

"Smells like shoe black," he said.

Toby was running in and out of the men. Bo came and flopped down at Caleb's feet and Toby took the opportunity for additional altitude and climbed up on Bo, reared up on his hind legs and bounced up and down, scratching at Caleb to get his attention.

The boy understood what the little dog wanted and leaned down to pick him up, at which point he began licking Caleb's face. Bo, watching the activity, snorted and laid his head back down, long ears flopping out next to him.

"I don't believe there's anything else to do and we may be messing things up for the sheriff. Let's all go to our houses. Mabel," he directed his attention to a woman in the crowd. "Since you live in the middle of the camp and everybody at your place has gone to town, why don't you let Miss Lydia stay with you tonight?"

She nodded in agreement and stepped forward to take the much younger woman by the arm. Several of the men looked at Mr. Gandy who nodded, and they left the crowd to escort the two women back to Mabel's house.

Caleb's daddy was still squatting and rubbing the sheet between his fingers as Caleb came over and knelt next to him.

"What's that on your face?" he asked his son, pointing.

Caleb reached up and rubbed the indicated spot.

"You're smearing it," Mr. Gandy said, wiping his son's face himself, then again smelling the fingers.

"What do you smell?"

"Dog, boy and shoe black. Did you get around this sheet?"

"No sir."

"Where'd it come from?" he mumbled to himself, looking around, his eyes finally settling on Toby, who was wriggling in Caleb's grasp. "Is that Miss Lydia's dog?"

"Yes sir."

Mr. Gandy reached over and took the dog from Caleb, then moved closer to the house where there was more light.

Caleb maneuvered to a spot where he could see better as his daddy lifted Toby level with his face.

"The damn dog's got it all over his muzzle too."

He handed the dog back to Caleb.

"Come on boy."

Caleb had to put Toby down so he could keep up with his daddy's long strides on the short walk back to camp. Toby and Bo ran back and forth and Caleb wished he had the time to watch them play, but it was all he could do to keep up, especially since the dogs' favorite playground was wherever his feet happened to be.

When they entered the edge of camp Mr. Gandy continued on straight instead of turning toward their house. Within a minute he was knocking on the Mabel White's door.

Miss Lydia opened the door.

"We thought we'd bring your dog to you."

"Thank you kindly Mr. Gandy. I'd forgot all about him."

"Didn't you say he tried to attack the man?"

"He did his best. Last I saw he was nipping at the man's face when he got tangled in the sheets and fell down."

"Thank you. There's going to be some men outside the house for the rest of the night so don't worry if you hear somebody walking around. We'll make sure you're safe."

"Thanks again."

CHAPTER 16

A Plan

The atmosphere around the camp was extremely tense. Miss Lydia had moved back to Shreveport after the sheriff had been unable to find any clues leading him to her attempted attacker. Children were being held close, even Caleb and Bo forced to forego the planned 'coon hunts because his mother forbade him to venture unaccompanied from the house after dark.

"But how are me and Bo supposed to win the blue ribbon if I don't get a chance to train him?" he'd argued.

"If you can't train him during the daylight or here at the house then I don't guess you will," she'd replied, finality in her tone.

Even an appeal to his father was unproductive.

"Sorry boy," Mr. Gandy had said. "She doesn't lay down the law very often, but when she does there ain't no use to argue."

He could still hunt during the day, but it wasn't the same. He'd put a sign up at the store saying he'd pay a dollar for a live 'coon but he'd taken it down a few days later after several people had asked him if he was trying to replace Johnny. Some of them had even made the remark in front of the boy, which riled Caleb and Leesie but which Johnny ignored.

"Don't it make you mad?" Caleb had asked him. Johnny shrugged.

"Even if it did, ain't nothing I can do about it. Better to ignore it and maybe they'll go on to somebody else."

When Joe Williams, a boy in their class, made a

similar remark Leesie punched him in the nose before Caleb had a chance. The other boy was so startled by the attack all he could do was run away, blood streaming from his nose and lips while Caleb took Leesie to the well to wash off her skinned knuckles.

"I don't see why you boys like fighting so much. I didn't even get hit and I'm still hurt," she said, shaking her hand in the air.

"Not as much as Joe though!" Caleb pantomimed someone boxing and threw a right jab. "Pow! Right in the kisser."

Both Leesie and Johnny giggled at Caleb as he bounced around swinging wildly.

It was one of the few times Johnny had smiled since the near attack on Miss Lydia. While all the black kids were looked down upon by most of the camp, Johnny was in a worse situation than the others because of who his daddy was.

"This camp is like a keg of gunpowder waiting for a spark," Mr. Gandy told his wife one night. "The longer we go without the sheriff catching somebody the more likely we are to have an explosion."

The firing of Ed Latham had both good and bad effects. While Ed was no longer sabotaging Luther at work and the men were no longer having to take up his slack when he was too drunk or too lazy to work, now he had time on his hands to gripe and stir things up among the men in the camp.

The general consensus among the white inhabitants, the only ones who counted, was that Luther Robinson was the likely attacker. This didn't change even after the sheriff let it be known that at the time of Miss Lydia's experience Luther was eating supper with his family and a neighbor who had dropped by.

"You can't believe nothing a nigger says," Ed Latham replied when presented with the alibi. "They all stick together. We're going to have to watch out for our women folks ourselves."

Even though the camp suspected Luther, few of

them were willing to do anything more than gossip about the possibility and distance themselves from him and his family. Caleb noticed Johnny had an ever increasing amount of free time, fewer people being willing to buy vegetables from a family tainted with not only the possibility of murder but also of race mixing, a moral crime almost as poorly thought of by most people as the killing.

The most vocal opponents of Luther Robinson were drawn to Ed Latham's circle as surely as iron filings are drawn to a magnet.

Although conversation about Luther would stop when Mr. Gandy was close, kids were often invisible to adults and Caleb heard the gossip of many of the naysayers, which grew progressively darker as weeks went by without an arrest.

One night Caleb snuck out his window to retrieve a pocket knife he'd suddenly remembered he'd left laying on Leesie's porch after a game of mumblety-peg with Ralph Foster. His path took him along the perimeter of a group of men, sitting around a fire sipping liquor.

"You see how the attacks stopped once't that nigger quit coming into camp so often?" Caleb heard Ed Latham's voice as he approached the fire, but still in the darkness. "But it's still just a matter of time until he does it again. Crazy 'coon like that can't help himself. He's no better than a rabid dog, needs to be put down."

Mumbles of assent greeted this observation.

"What exactly are you proposing Ed?" a voice from the other side of the fire asked. Caleb knew from the way the words were slurred the man had been drinking for a while.

"It seems to me," Ed took a break and sipped from a Mason jar. "That we aren't real men if we can't protect our women."

Another voice spoke up. "Your woman left, Ed."

"Kiss my ass," Ed snarled back at his

antagonist. "I'm not talking about any particular woman, just women in general."

"So, again, what are you proposing we do?"

"I think we ought to do a little night riding. My grandpa used to tell me how they handled uppity niggers after the war. A good scare might be just what Luther Robinson needs to show him he's not wanted around here."

"What about his wife and kid?"

"A pickaninny is a pickaninny," Ed replied.

"I'm not having anything to do with this," a man said. Caleb couldn't see the speaker, but did see a jar of moonshine fly through the air and smash against the timbers that made up the fire, causing it to flare up and the men to step back from the flames. The man left, followed by a couple of others.

Ed sensed his followers losing interest in taking action if Dora and Johnny might be harmed.

"Now that the cowards are gone I can say that of course we're not going to harm the woman or boy," he paused then added, "leastways, not as long as they don't interfere."

"So when do we do this?"

"Tomorrow night, no need to waste time. Meet up east of camp on the trail by the lightning struck pine a half hour after dark. Bring sheets, a torch, hoods, and guns."

"We walking?"

"Hell no. Bring horses. If'n you ain't got a horse, borrow a mule. Hell, I'll even spring for the liquor."

"What? Ed Latham buying a drink? I'd come just for that."

The sound of men's laughter helped cover any noise Caleb made as he slipped away from the men and started running to his house.

Within a few seconds he realized he had made an error. He stopped running and was extricating himself from a sawbriar wrapped around his legs when

114

he heard someone pushing through the brush behind him.

Rather than continuing to carefully pick the briars loose he just grunted and ran, feeling the sharp pain as the thorns made shallow cuts in his legs before they finally ripped free of his clothing. He heard his pursuer getting closer and put on a burst of speed just as he saw the pale light from his house through a break in the trees. He heard the footsteps quicken behind him and his heart jumped as he imagined a hand suddenly seizing him from behind.

He was just about to yell for his father when his foot caught on a root and he fell, knocking his breath from his body. Before he could recover something struck him, and he blacked out.

****

"Caleb! Caleb! Are you all right?"

Caleb slowly regained consciousness and realized Leesie had his cheeks grasped firmly in her hands, occasionally letting go to slap him.

"Quit hitting me Leesie! I'm fine!"

Caleb pushed her off of him, got to his feet and then grabbed her under her arms to help her up.

"What were you following me for?"

"I left my doll outside and while I was looking for her I saw you creeping around the fire. When I heard what they were planning I lit out to tell your daddy, but I saw you ahead of me and was trying to catch up when I fell over you. I thought I'd killed you for a second."

"You nearly did. You been eating rocks?" Caleb rubbed his ribs where Leesie had landed.

"Hush. What are we gonna do? What if they hurt Johnny? Or his parents?"

"Daddy will know what to do," Caleb said with certainty.

****

"I'm not sure what to do," Mr. Gandy said.

Caleb and Leesie had burst through the door of the cabin, startling both Bo and Mr. Gandy from their napping positions, the man in his chair and the dog stretched out next to him, a bone nestled between his oversized front paws. He awoke with a yelp and a leap to one side, the jump knocking the heavy bone onto Mr. Gandy's foot causing him to jump up and hop around on one foot until the pain subsided.

Normally the events would have caused both Caleb and Leesie to erupt in laughter, but instead a torrent of words began pouring from their mouths, worry about Johnny and his family as well as the adrenaline from the run through the woods causing them to talk over each other.

"Whoa! Calm down!" Mr. Gandy paused from rubbing his foot to hold up a hand. "What's got you two so excited?" He sat back down on his chair.

Mrs. Gandy peeked around the door from the kitchen.

"Caleb? Leesie? What are you two doing out after dark?"

They both started talking again, but Leesie was the calmer of the two and reached over, putting her hand over Caleb's mouth and stifling the babble.

"Mr. Gandy, we just heard Ed Latham and some of the other men talking about going over to the Robinson's house with guns and torches. They said they were going to teach Mr. Robinson a lesson."

Caleb's daddy leapt to his feet again and started looking for his shoes.

"How long ago was it? Were they getting ready to leave then?"

"It was just a few minutes ago, but they aren't going until tomorrow after dark." Caleb had pulled Leesie's hand from his mouth, and started sputtering and spitting after he finished talking. She still had a

116

healthy dose of dirt on her hand from the fall in the woods and had ground it into his lips when she'd stopped him from talking.

"Good, that gives me some time. Caleb, you wash up and go to bed...and stay there. Leesie, I'll walk you home."

He slipped his boots on, wincing, and walked to the door, holding it open for Leesie. Bo perked up his ears as if interested in following, but when Caleb headed for his room he trailed along behind him instead. Mrs. Gandy did as well, stopping only when her husband stuck his head back in the door.

"Abigail, you don't fuss at him for going out. He usually minds and this minor hitch may have saved someone's life or at least the Robinson's house."

Caleb's mother pursed her lips, but returned to the kitchen.

Caleb, who had been sure he was about to get punished, looked at his dad, who winked at him.

"Not again," he said in warning.

"Yes sir. I mean, no sir."

The screen door slammed behind him and Leesie and a few minutes later Caleb was in bed, Bo stretched out next to him on the floor.

He was too excited to sleep right away, so he was still awake and heard the door slam when his father returned from Leesie's.

The low drone of his parent's talking combined with the reassuring sounds of Bo's snoring eventually lulled him to sleep.

CHAPTER 17

Night Riders

Mr. Gandy's footsteps awoke Caleb the next morning. Just as he pulled his shoes on he heard the screen door slam and the sound of his father walking across the front porch. He and Bo shot from the bedroom door, pausing long enough to grab a couple of biscuits from a dishcloth covered plate on the kitchen table. Before Mr. Gandy had gotten ten steps out of the yard the boy was at his heels, eating his biscuit and tossing pieces to Bo.

"Where you headed?"

"I'm going to the store to call the sheriff on Mr. Jenkins's new telephone." The camp had been abuzz when Mr. Jenkins had the machinery installed a few weeks before. The excitement had quickly died down when people realized no one they knew had a telephone, so the odd looking contraption remained a curiosity rather than a convenience, people gathering at the store anytime the bell was heard ringing.

The man who had installed the telephone explained to everyone about how the lines had to be run from Natchitoches to the camp, and to Caleb it hardly seemed worth the trouble. Many inhabitants opined that it was too much trouble to ever catch on in a big way. Caleb agreed with that, but it was still exciting to hear it ring and hear a voice coming from nearly thirty miles away that sounded like it was just across the yard.

Caleb spotted Leesie skipping through camp.

"Hey Leesie," he hollered at her.

"What'cha doing?" she asked as she ran up to them.

"Going to the store to call the sheriff," Caleb said, his chest swelling out a little with the importance of the task.

"Hush now," Mr. Gandy said to them. "Y'all can come with me. But you need to stay quiet and out of the way. If they hear about me calling the sheriff they'll just call it off for tonight and do it some other time. The Robinsons might not have any warning then."

"We'll be quiet," Caleb assured him, Leesie nodding in agreement. No way were they going to take a chance of missing something that exciting.

The two kids followed Mr. Gandy into the store, quietly standing to one side. Bo took up his usual position on the porch, body squarely blocking the door and nose close to the crack where he could catch a stray whiff of Caleb's scent even though he couldn't see him.

The building was unoccupied except for the storekeeper. Mr. Gandy spoke to him in low tones while Caleb and Leesie wandered the aisles, gnawing on pieces of licorice Mr. Jenkins had retrieved from a glass jar on the counter and handed to them, all the while keeping up his side of the conversation.

"Just pick up the ear piece and hold it to your ear," Mr. Jenkins instructed. "Crank that little lever on the side a few times. A woman's voice is going to answer and then you just tell her you want the sheriff and she'll connect you. I'll stand over by the door and make sure nobody comes in."

Caleb thought his daddy looked much more comfortable swinging a double bit axe in the middle of the woods than he did in the store hunched over and yelling into the mouthpiece of the telephone.

"You don't need to holler quite so loud," Mr. Jenkins offered. "They can hear you fine if you talk normal, just put your mouth in front of the mouthpiece."

After a few minutes he put the earpiece back in the holder and Mr. Jenkins came from his post at the screen door and took up his usual position behind the

119

counter.

"What'd he say?"

"He's not going to be able to help us. He's got to go to Winnfield and won't make it back by tonight."

"So what do you do?"

"He said to do what I think is necessary, but he can't arrest anybody until they actually commit a crime. He suggested we get a few men together and be at the Robinson's house tonight when the other men get there. If anything bad happens he said we could consider ourselves deputized as of right now."

"George, I'd love to help Luther out, but I don't think I'd be willing to shoot at anybody from the camp. Not unless they were shooting at me."

"I understand, Dan. It probably wouldn't be good for business if it got out that you'd sided with Luther against the white folks. It wouldn't take but a match or two to put you out of business. I'll round up help elsewhere. I *can* count on you to stay quiet?"

"Of course, of course."

Mr. Gandy touched a finger to the brim of his hat and left the building, Leesie and Caleb trailing behind.

"Leesie, you go on to your house, Caleb and me has some walking to do and I don't think it's proper for a young lady to come with us."

"Yes sir," she responded, waved at Caleb and took off running for her house, blonde hair flying behind her.

His daddy turned without speaking and started walking through camp. He stopped at a cabin Caleb knew belong to a Cajun named LeFleur. Two big scars on his face created a fearsome expression, but Caleb knew the man had a soft heart and always had a piece of candy for him and a piece of beef jerky for Bo.

LeFleur worked the night shift, rendering turpentine from the pine trees. He answered the knock at his door wiping sleep from his eyes. Even from where he was standing just off the porch, Caleb could smell the strong pine scent wafting from him. It didn't appear to bother Bo though, as the dog was sniffing at the man's pockets, tail wagging in anticipation of the usual treat.

"George," LeFleur said in acknowledgment when he opened the door.

"Raymond," Mr. Gandy said. "Would it be all right if I came in for a minute?"

"Sure," LeFleur said in his thick accent. "I'll start a pot of coffee. Caleb coming in with you?"

"No, it'd probably be better if he waited out here."

"Suit yourself," LeFleur held the door open, blocking Bo from entering with his foot. He nodded at Caleb and winked.

His daddy was only inside a little while, long enough for Caleb to find an appropriate whittling stick and get started. He'd carve a minute, then throw a stick for Bo to fetch. The fetching part was easy, but getting the stick back from the dog always involved a wrestling match.

Eventually the door opened and his daddy reappeared, LeFleur right behind him.

"About 5?"

"That ought to be good. I'll get Ukiah, and you get a couple of others. That ought to be enough."

"I know Riley will want to go. Ed cut him last year after Riley thought they'd finished their fight. He'd have killed him then if I hadn't stopped him."

"I don't want any shooting unless it's absolutely necessary and no killing at all. Be sure and tell Riley that. He'll get a chance to embarrass Latham, but we're acting as deputies tonight and that means no shooting at all unless we're shot at first."

LeFleur scratched his head and grinned.

"I'll tell him. He won't like it much, but he'll listen."

The man stuck his hand in his pocket and flipped a piece of candy to Caleb. A similar flip and Bo caught the offering out of the air.

"Thanks," Caleb said.

The man waved as he shut the door.

"I'll be at Ukiah's for a while," his daddy said. "Do you want to come with me or go on and play with your friends?"

"I'll go with you. It'll give Bo a chance to visit his momma."

"Fair enough. If you happen to overhear anything you're not supposed to, you keep it to yourself. Remember, it's men talk and not to be shared with your momma or anybody else, even Leesie."

"Yes sir."

The walk to Ukiah's was more difficult than usual, since the heat and a wetter than usual summer had allowed the briars and weeds to explode with new growth, occasionally blocking the path and requiring them to watch their footing. A foot snagging on a vine could mean a slide and tumble in the loose dirt and gravel. Still, it was a beautiful morning. The temperature was still in the comfortable range just barely hinting at the oncoming fall, and the stifling summer heat was fading. In Louisiana, heat was never far away but the fall and winter would provide at least as many cool days as hot ones.

Bo had bolted for Ukiah's house when they reached the bottom of the hill. As the two approached they could hear the sound of mock growling and combat as he tussled with the sole remaining sibling under the watchful, but bored, gaze of his mother. A few puppies from the latest litter tried to join in, and the yips as they were knocked flying could be heard above the din.

"Howdy George, Caleb," Ukiah said as they approached. He was locking the shed that held his supply of moonshine.

"Mornin' Ukiah. At work already?"

"Just locking up. Had a customer this morning bought a half dozen jars. Must be planning a shindig."

122

"Do you mind if I ask who it was?"

"Ed Latham."

"No surprise there. Did he mention why he needed so much?"

"Nope. Got a little hot under the collar when I asked too. Got even hotter when I mentioned he might want to save his money now that he was unemployed."

"I hadn't thought of that. Ed must have squirreled away some money. Not like him, he usually spent it as fast as he could make it. Jenkins said he paid off his bill at the store and paid a couple of months rent in advance."

"He come into some money somewhere, had a pocketful of something that jingled. I saw a gold piece, a wad of bills, and a few silver dollars when he paid me."

"Hmmm." Caleb's daddy stared off into space for a few seconds.

"So what brings you here?" Ukiah's question interrupted the pondering.

"Expecting a little trouble over to Luther Robinson's tonight from Ed and his cohorts, likely fueled by your liquor. Thought you might be willing to lend a hand and maybe change their mind once't they get there."

"Not going to get in any trouble with the law am I?"

"Not for this, already got the sheriff's okay."

"I sure do like Luther and his family. Little Johnny brought me a big plate of fried pies last week. Least I could do would be to help scare off a bunch of bullies. Count me in."

"If Ed and his boys recognize you it might be bad for business."

"Some things are more important than money. Besides, where else are they gonna get liquor out here? It ain't like creek water is a good substitute. I imagine I can still scratch out a living even if they are mad at me."

"Get to Luther's before dark and take a back way there, that way Latham's boys won't notice a bunch of tracks and get scared off. Of course, they'll likely be too drunk to notice anything, but I don't want to take any chances. I'd rather handle it once and for all tonight than have to worry about it popping up again."

"I expect that'd be best. When you've got a skunk in your sights, take the shot or he'll be back to raid the hen house another night."

Mr. Gandy held out his hand.

"I appreciate the help."

The two men shook hands.

"Like I said, least I can do to thank them for that plate of fried pies."

Another stream of tobacco juice from each man sealed the deal and Caleb, after a final tousle of his hair by Ukiah, was headed back down the hill behind his father.

"Caleb!" Ukiah's yell stopped him.

"Yes sir?"

"Bo's been spending a lot of time up here lately. Comes up here to play with the new puppies. He's not any bother, but if'n you ever get to looking for him you may want to check up here."

"Yes sir. If he gets to be trouble let me know and I'll tie him up."

"That dog's got too much spirit to be tied up for long. He's always welcome here."

"Thanks Ukiah. I'd better scoot, Daddy's getting pretty far ahead."

A whistle and the 'coon dog exploded over the top of the hill and collided with the boy. They tumbled to the bottom, then took off at a run to catch up to Mr. Gandy.

"Can I come with you tonight?"

Caleb knew the answer before he asked, but figured it was worth a shot.

"Afraid not son. Things have a way of getting out of hand, particularly with guns, liquor and stupid people being involved. I'm gonna head on over to Luther's and send Dora and Johnny back here to stay the night. Y'all need to stay inside though."

Usually not averse to politely arguing to get his way, Caleb knew that even if his daddy agreed to let him go, no amount of arguing or whining would ever get the mission approved by his mother, so he'd save the effort for another time when there was a better chance of success.

The day crawled by, his daddy appearing and disappearing occasionally. A few men dropped by the house, spoke with Mr. Gandy for a few minutes in low tones, and left.

Following one extended absence he suddenly reappeared among the trees behind the house, Dora and Johnny Robinson trailing behind. He hurried them across the back porch and into the house before anyone could see. Even Bo, normally excited at the arrival of visitors, was restrained, not barking or causing any commotion.

About an hour before dark Mr. Gandy walked into the living room where his wife and Dora Robinson sat shelling peas into big metal pans held across their laps. Dora's mother sat napping in a rocker to the side and Caleb and Johnny were on the floor, building things out of blocks before knocking them back down with a clatter.

"We're fixin' to leave," he said. "I don't expect any trouble here, but I'm leaving a man outside just in case."

"You be careful," his wife said, then hugged him quickly. The glint of a tear showed in the corner of her eye, but a quick wipe with the corner of her apron cleared it.

"Thank you Mr. Gandy," Dora Robinson said. "Ain't many folks, black or white, that'd look out for us the way you do."

"I'd like to think you're wrong about that Dora, but even if you're right, that'll change with time."

He nodded once to Caleb and walked out the door, toting his rifle in one hand and a box of bullets in the other. Caleb could hear the creak of the saddle leather as he swung onto his horse. A few seconds later he could hear the horse and rider enter the woods behind the house. Caleb knew that all over camp other men were doing the same. In a half an hour or so another group of men would be leaving the camp, the same ones who were now clustered together in Ed Latham's house sipping the clear liquor from fruit jars, imbibing liquid courage.

The Gandy's house, like the rest of the camp, was unusually quiet that night. A storm had rolled through a little earlier, and it had started sprinkling rain. Word had spread of the planned activities and, while the rest of the inhabitants of the camp didn't pick a side, or even know that the Robinson's had anyone backing them, everyone waited in hushed households for what they believed was the predetermined outcome.

In the Gandy house, everybody watched the clock on the mantle. At about 9:30, the distant sound of gunfire could be heard and both Mrs. Gandy and Mrs. Robinson leapt to their feet and ran to the front porch, worry evident on their faces. Their concern spread to their sons and Caleb found himself standing at the screen door, feeling like his heart was in his throat.

About thirty minutes after the last shot, Caleb heard a small group of horses ride into camp at breakneck speed. No other noises could be heard but the rate at which the riders dispersed indicated they wouldn't be celebrating any actions they'd taken that night.

Soon after, more horses could be heard and Bo started barking just before the front gate could be heard opening and closing.

The screen door burst open before anyone could get to their feet and Luther Robinson strode through, supporting Mr. Gandy who had blood evident on the upper part of his chest. Ukiah followed them into the room carrying two guns.

"Oh my lord!" Abigail Gandy exclaimed, rushing to her husband.

Caleb's daddy grimaced in pain as Luther helped him into a chair.

"Don't panic Abigail, it looks lots worse that it is," he said to his wife from between clenched teeth.

Luther helped Mrs. Gandy remove his shirt, a groan escaping the wounded man's lips as he twisted to allow the garment to be peeled back, and Caleb saw a hole between the collarbone and the shoulder begin to bleed as the dried blood was peeled back with the shirt.

"Y'all best get some water boiling and some clean cloths. One of the men is fetching Doc Sanders," Ukiah said, keeping a watch through the door. After a minute he yelled outside.

"Keep 'em tied up. If they try anything just shoot 'em."

Caleb and Johnny peeked out a front window and saw three men clad in white sheets sitting on the ground with their backs against the oak tree. Each had their arms tied to their sides and another rope connected them all together. Two other men stood over them, pistols held loosely in their hands. Occasionally they'd spit a stream of tobacco juice, close enough to the prisoners that their sheets were splashed each time.

"Sure you don't want me to just shoot 'em anyway?" Even though the speaker's face was obscured by the dark, the heavy accent clearly marked him as LeFleur.

"Nah, not just yet, although the son of a bitches deserve it," Ukiah responded.

The men on the ground looked at each other nervously but, deciding discretion was the better part of valor, remained silent.

More steps on the front porch signaled the arrival of the doctor. Ukiah opened the screen door to let him in. He started rolling up his sleeves as soon as he saw the wound.

127

"Tsk, tsk, tsk," he clucked at Mr. Gandy. "I thought you had better sense than to stand in front of where a bullet wanted to go."

"I thought I did too. I must be slowing down in my old age."

"Fetch me a pan and clean cloths Abigail," the doctor said as he pulled a stool in front of Mr. Gandy's chair and leaned forward to look at the wound. After a few seconds he stood and moved to examine the man's back.

"Well, as bullet wounds go you got a good one. It's a through and through, which means I don't get to have the fun of digging around in there to get the bullet out. It missed all the bones, but it's still going to hurt a mite when I clean it out. Maybe that'll teach you to use better sense."

He flipped his satchel open and took out some bandages and a couple of shiny instruments.

Caleb and Johnny were standing together and to one side of the adults. He felt Johnny bump into him as he swayed a little bit when the doctor poked at the edges of the wound, causing the blood to flow again.

"What's the matter?" Caleb asked him in a whisper, trying not to catch the attention of the adults.

"Just hot I guess. I feel all squirmy inside."

"Well, be still before they shoo us out of here."

Doc Sanders took a piece of the cloth, held it with one of the shiny tools and poured a strong smelling liquid over it.

"Put some of these towels in his lap and behind him. He's liable to bleed a bit."

As the doctor leaned over and jammed the cloth into the bullet hole Mr. Gandy let out a gasp and grabbed the arm of his chair. Simultaneously with the gasp was a loud 'thump' drawing the adults' attention to the area occupied by the boys.

Caleb, while wincing in sympathy for his dad, was still watching with curiosity.

As he noticed the adults looking in his direction

128

he shrugged.

"He passed out," he said, bumping Johnny's prostrate form with his foot. "I guess it was too much excitement for one night."

CHAPTER 18

London Bridge

The doctor gave Mr. Gandy an injection which he said would put him to sleep but before it took effect he, along with Luther Robinson and Ukiah, filled the rest of them in on what had happened.

"When we got there, me and Ukiah went inside but the rest of the fellows took to the woods to wait for Latham's bunch. We could hear them coming way before we got there so we doused the lights to make them think the Robinsons had went to bed. It was actually kind of funny watching them out in the yard, the bed sheets flapping around, rain coming down, them too drunk to control their horses. They'd dragged a big cross soaked in kerosene through the woods but were too drunk to stand it up and apparently nobody had thought about bringing a shovel to dig a hole to sink the base of it in. Somebody set it on fire and it started burning on the ground but it spooked the horses and they threw a couple of them off, so those men had to run off chasing after their rides."

He paused for a second, shifted positions and grimaced. After a sip from the coffee cup offered by his wife he continued the story.

"Finally, Latham started hollering for Luther to come out of the house and they shot their guns up in the air a few times. At that point our guys in the woods started shooting and things got even more confusing. Half the fellows in sheets started hightailing it back to camp, the ones tied up outside fell off their horses and were grabbed, but at least one of the others fired a shot or two at the house. The shooter was riding what looked like Latham's horse, but I couldn't swear to it. One of those shots is the one that nicked me."

"What happened next?" Caleb asked.

"Well, Luther stepped out onto the porch with that double barreled shotgun of his and hollered 'Y'all looking' for me?' just before he fired both barrels. When those blasts went off and they saw Luther calmly walking through the yard toward them, shotgun ready, they turned tail and ran."

"You chased them off daddy?" Johnny asked, beaming.

"I don't know about all that," Luther said.

"Oh, don't let him fool you Johnny. Your daddy stepped right into the midst of them. There was one fellow with a torch riding toward the house and your daddy knocked him off the horse with the stock of his shotgun. The leader turned to ride off and caught both barrels in his backside."

"You killed him?" Johnny asked.

"Naw, I had my gun loaded with rock salt. It wouldn't kill a cat."

"But he'll have a problem sitting down for a while," Mr. Gandy said with a laugh. "I expect we'll know who he was pretty quick. Just look for the man who stands through church service."

"They did tear the house up some though," Luther said.

"How bad is it?" Dora asked, worry clear in her voice and on her face.

"Somebody rode their horse up onto the porch and knocked the railing down and dropped their torch. The boards caught fire."

"My lord!" Abigail Gandy said, putting her arms around Dora.

"Don't fret," Mr. Gandy told Dora. "We got the fire put out pretty quick. I'll send a crew over there tomorrow morning and they'll have it fixed by lunch time. It may still smell a little smoky, but it'll be fixed."

"Bless you," Dora said.

131

"We want y'all to stay here tonight, too. Just in case," Abigail said.

"We'd hate to put y'all out any more," Luther responded. "Y'all have done too much already."

"Nonsense, Dora and Mrs. Gaskey can sleep in Caleb's bed, you can sleep on the couch and the boys can bunk on a pallet on the back porch," Abigail insisted.

"Sure, then we'll get the crew together in the morning and get your supplies from the store."

Caleb's daddy stifled a yawn, the medicine starting to make him sleepy.

"Luther, tell Ukiah and the rest to take those boys and tie them to the tree in front of the blacksmith's shop. Anyone who stands guard on 'em tonight can have tomorrow and the next day off with pay."

Luther stepped to the door as Caleb's mother disappeared into the back room, reappearing a few moments later with a bundle of blankets and quilts.

"Let's get the boys bedded down," Abigail said to Dora.

Caleb poked Johnny in the ribs.

"Let's make a couple of sandwiches and we'll pretend we're camping out."

Johnny nodded in agreement.

"Cake too?"

"Cake too."

Bo wagged his tail in agreement.

****

While Mr. Gandy fell asleep, the other adults stayed up talking for quite a while. For both the Robinsons and Mrs. Gandy it was a rare chance to visit with people in a social setting, without the stigma normally associated with such activity between the races. They learned, as their children had learned months earlier, that the differences in the people were small and the difference in culture could be celebrated

132

without being demeaned.

The boys, along with Bo of course, awakened the next morning to wonderful smells drifting from the kitchen. The smells hadn't been responsible for them waking up, a distant crash of thunder had done that, but the prospect of a good breakfast propelled them and the dog from their quilts.

Their fathers were sitting at the kitchen table sipping on cups of coffee, the empty plates from their breakfast already swept away, washed and dried, and returned to the table for the use of their sons. Mr. Gandy's left arm was in a sling, the white of a bandage showing through the open collar of his shirt.

The boys gorged themselves on biscuits, bacon, ham and eggs. Bo was the lucky recipient of not only the food that fell to the floor, but also the occasional morsel snuck from the table and slipped to him.

"If you boys will hurry up and finish you can go to the store with us," Mr. Gandy said, "Who knows? There may even be a treat in it for you if you help us load the wagon."

"Can Leesie help too?" Caleb asked.

"Sure. Y'all run and get her while we hitch the wagon. We'll meet you at the store."

They took off in a flash. Johnny purposely held back to make it appear to be more of a race than it really was. Caleb's slight limp, the remnant of the hog hunt, meant his days of foot racing were over but Johnny couldn't bear to hurt his feelings. Bo loped ahead then turned around to race in circles around them, happiness at being with his boy filling him to the brim.

Leesie heard them coming and met them before they got to her house.

"I've been about to explode from curiosity. What happened last night?"

"We're going to meet our dads at the store. Come with us and we'll tell you about it on the way."

The three ambled toward the store, Johnny and Leesie both walking at Caleb's pace.

By the time they arrived at the store the story had been recounted, although there had been a brief tussle when Caleb had explained about Johnny fainting, despite Johnny's unsuccessful struggles to clamp his hand over the bigger boy's mouth.

They quieted down and stopped all foolishness when they got to the store. The wagon was parked in front of it and a horse was tied at the rail. The children walked quietly into the store and stepped to the side, taking a moment to shake off the dampness their clothes had accumulated during the walk through the misty rain.

Johnny was the first to notice the owner of the horse standing to one side of the counter. He poked Caleb in the arm and nodded toward where Ed Latham stood, staring daggers at the other men, who were ignoring him. Mr. Robinson strode quietly to the hardware section of the store, looking over nails and other equipment necessary to rebuild the portions of the house damaged by the fire.

"...and the sorry sons of bitches were a sight," Mr. Gandy was saying to the storekeeper.

"Did you recognize any of them?" Mr. Jenkins asked.

"Just the ones we caught. I expect the sheriff will be able to get them to talk though. He'll likely have them all within a day or two."

Mr. Jenkins looked distinctly uncomfortable about discussing the previous night's events in front of Ed Latham. Mr. Gandy, however, had no such qualms. Caleb could tell from his red ears that his dad was mad.

"You should have seen the cowards scatter when Luther let loose with his shotgun. Whoever the leader was, he'll be sitting funny for a while."

Caleb could see Latham's hands clenching and unclenching on the counter. He took a few steps toward the front of the store, a limp clearly visible, before turning back to the storekeeper. A look of pain twisted his face at the sudden turn.

134

"If y'all are finished yakking, can I get the rest of my things?"

"Sure Ed, sure. Be right back George."

The storekeeper pulled several boxes from behind the counter and stacked them on top. He added a handful of tobacco plugs, a box of bullets, and a few other items. Ed Latham grabbed them and dropped them into a burlap bag he was carrying.

"In a hurry Ed?" Mr. Gandy asked.

"A mite. I've got to go to Natchitoches today."

"Is that right? Riding your horse there?"

"Not that it's any of your business, but yes I am why"

"If you hang around a while the sheriff might give you a ride in his truck. He's got a few other people he's going to be taking there."

Latham's face turned bright red as he turned back to Mr. Jenkins and snarled, "Hurry up!"

"Easy now Ed, hold your horses. The train's always late anyway."

"Catching a train are you Ed?"

"Yeah. Going to see my brother," he started digging in his pocket. "That's good enough. How much do I owe you?"

As Mr. Jenkins began figuring up the bill, Ed pulled a pocket watch out and flipped it open. A tinny sound could dimly be heard as he looked at the time.

Caleb felt a poke in his ribs and looked at Leesie.

"Caleb! The watch! Can you hear it? It's playing London Bridge!" Leesie whispered.

He focused his attention on the watch rather than the man and realized Leesie was right. Now that he was paying attention he could see that what he had thought was a long piece of string attached at the top was actually a cord made of braided, blonde hair.

He stepped forward and tugged on his daddy's pants leg.

"Not now," he said, slapping gently at Caleb's

hand.

"Daddy! Now!" Caleb urged.

Mr. Gandy allowed himself to be led to where the children were and squatted down.

"What is it?"

"The watch Daddy! The watch! It belonged to Miss Callie."

"Are you sure?"

"I'm sure. I told you about it, remember? The cord was made from her daughter's hair!"

Caleb looked at Leesie, who nodded.

"Y'all stay back," Mr. Gandy stood and used his free arm to push Caleb behind him, then walked back to the counter.

"Nice watch Ed," he said.

"Thank you" Ed said it in response to Mr. Gandy's statement, but the tone and his actions made it clear it was an instinctual response. He rested his hand on his knife as he lifted the sack of supplies with the other hand.

"It's funny. I should have known that the loudest mouth would have been the first place to look."

"What are you talking about?" Latham asked as he edged around the counter, his back now to the front door, the counter between him and the other two men.

"It never occurred to me that somebody might put shoe polish on their face to make someone think a black man was after them. You never intended to hurt Lydia, you just wanted her to think a black man was trying to attack her. Once they decided who had done it, you wouldn't have to worry about them poking around anymore would you? Get rid of a man you hated and put yourself in the clear at the same time."

He didn't receive a reply, and leaned over to reach for something under the counter.

"What happened Ed? Did Callie turn you down because you didn't have any money? Or were you too liquored up to perform?"

Mr. Gandy suddenly stood, a rifle in his hand.

136

Unfortunately, the rifle was a little longer than he thought and the front sight caught on the underside of the counter. Before he could clear it, Latham swung the sack of supplies, crashing into the wounded shoulder and causing Mr. Gandy to cry out in pain and drop the rifle. Ed whipped his knife out and took a step toward the counter but a sudden 'crack' sounded as Luther Robinson swung the axe handle he'd grabbed from a barrel when he'd silently entered. The piece of wood missed Latham's arm, but hit the knife knocking it from his hand.

With a scream of fury, Latham wheeled and feinted toward the kids, but when Luther jumped in that direction Ed ran past him and out the front door of the store. He jumped onto his horse, which began to buck and snort. The noise woke Bo from his sleeping position on the porch, and he began to bark frantically, the noise causing the horse to become even more panicked. As the other men burst onto the front porch Ed was thrown from the horse, landing on his back side in the mud, then scrambled to his feet, grabbed his rifle from its sheath on the saddle of the frightened horse, and ran into the woods behind the store.

Caleb's daddy grabbed Luther by the arm to stop him from following.

"Let him go," he said. "The Sheriff'll be here soon. There's no need to give him an easy chance to kill one of us."

The two men walked back to calm the horse before he hurt himself rearing and bucking.

"Caleb! Get your dog!"

"Bo!"

At the command the dog ran up the steps to sit next to Caleb, tail wagging at the great fun in which he had been involved. He didn't mind being called back since horses were playthings, not to be confused with his real prey, raccoons. No one could have called him off of a raccoon trail.

Luther took the horse by the bridle, steadying

137

his head and neck and pulling him close to scratch and whisper to him until he calmed down. Mr. Gandy reached into one of the boxes of supplies that had already been loaded onto the wagon and withdrew an apple which he gently tossed to Luther. As the horse contentedly munched on the treat, the two men examined him.

"Look here," Mr. Gandy said. He wiped his hand on the horse's flank and showed them a sheen of blood on it.

"And here." He pointed at the back of the saddle.

From his position on the porch Caleb could see small, dark marks peppering the leather.

"What is it daddy?"

"Looks to me like where a load of rock salt hit. I'd say we not only found Callie's killer but confirmed who the man was that led the charge last night."

Caleb reached out and gently stroked the horse's flank, then looked at the blood on his hand. As he watched, the rain increased, washing the blood off of his hand and onto the ground.

CHAPTER 19

The Flood

The rain continued to fall for a week, with no sign of letting up. Folks from the camp began walking to Kisatchie Creek every day, measuring its rise with a series of sticks driven into the ground. Everyone knew the creek was prone to flood every ten years or so, covering the hollows and bottoms of the forest with rich, brown water, uprooting trees and lives.

After the week of water, Mr. Gandy received word from the company to close the camp down until the danger had passed. He packed up the sawmill equipment and most of the goods from the store and sent it into Natchitoches.

All over the camp people were filling wagons with as much of their lives as they could, canvas tarps stretched over meager loads to prevent any further drenching.

The inhabitants of Turpentine Camp #3 would leave in a procession, so that when the inevitable wagon bogged down in the mud there'd be plenty of help to get it back on the evacuation trail.

"You packed up?" Mr. Gandy asked Caleb as they tied down the last of the furniture. "Got your rod and reel?"

"Yes sir. Everything's packed. Should I go help Leesie?"

"No, you better stay here. I sent two of the single men to make sure Leesie and her momma got packed up nice and neat and to drive their wagon. They'll be fine."

He looked around.

"Where's Bo?"

"I don't know. I've been looking for him all morning."

"You'd better find him. We'll be leaving in a quick-get-ready."

"Yes sir."

Caleb's whistling and yelling yielded no results.

"You better go find him," his daddy said. "But hurry. I don't want to have to hold the whole camp up on account of that fool dog."

Caleb took off as fast as his limp would allow. He ran through the camp whistling and yelling Bo's name. Each time he passed somebody he'd ask if they'd seen the dog, but each question he just received a "Nope" with no pause in their packing. The people were in a hurry to leave since the small creek behind Johnny's house was now a raging torrent, growing by the hour and the entire camp was awash with rain water running off the hills surrounding it. While the delay wasn't likely to result in any lost lives, the dirt roads had already turned into quagmires and could easily result in a wagon load of personal belongings being abandoned if it bogged down and couldn't be freed.

Caleb knew if Bo had been in ear shot he would have come when he heard the yells, so he knew the next logical place to check was Ukiah's house.

The climb up the hill was even more difficult than usual since the rain water was pouring down the now muddy trail. He slipped and fell a few times, the twinge in his leg telling him that he was pushing as hard as he could.

The hilltop was quiet. None of the puppies could be seen and the chicken coop was empty.

He started to knock when he noticed a note sticking out from the doorjamb.

Dear Caleb,
I left in a hurry, since the weather is supposed to be even worse south of here. I'm going to

140

Alexandria and stay with that voodoo woman I told you about. I'll likely be back as soon as the weather clears up. Take care of your friends and give Bo a big lick for me.
See you soon.
Your friend,
Ukiah

Caleb folded the note and stuck it into his pocket, then whistled and yelled a few times for Bo before walking around back to the cane press in case the dog was there.

He didn't see any sign of Bo, but the door to Ukiah's moonshine shed was swinging in the wind, slamming back against the building with each gust. He decided to latch it and took a few steps in that direction when a man suddenly stepped from the shed, head down so his hat protected his face from the rain.

"Ukiah!" Caleb yelled, glad for a chance to tell the old man goodbye in person.

The figure slowly raised his head to look Caleb in the eye.

It was Ed Latham, a jug of whiskey in one hand and his rifle in the other.

****

A sneer appeared on Latham's face.

"Howdy Mr. Latham, have you seen my dog?" Caleb asked, bravely trying to keep his voice from shaking.

The man slowly shook his head from side to side, then lifted the jug of whiskey and took a sip.

Caleb began to back up but the man edged sideways and cut off the route back to the safety of the camp.

His lips curled as he said two words, "Nigger lover."

Caleb jerked left, the sudden move causing

another twinge to shoot through the leg savaged in the hog hunt. As the man moved in the direction he'd feinted, Caleb ran right, toward the edge of the hill. Just as he reached it he dodged right again, aiming for a cleared stretch of hillside, but in the direction away from the camp.

The move likely saved his life. He heard the sharp crack of the rifle then a buzz as the bullet went past him. Rather than try and run down the hill Caleb launched himself into a clear patch and landed on the seat of his pants. The wet pine straw combined with the mud underneath to send him on a wild slide, occasionally slowed as he hit a rock jutting from the hillside. Whether by providence or luck he made it to the bottom of the hill in record time, scrambling to his feet and running toward the river, the sound of the man a ways behind him but getting louder as the distance was closed.

Caleb was hoping to head toward the river, then cut back and follow it to a trail leading to the camp. Blundering into the forest in this rain might result in either getting lost or trapped between the man with the rifle and an impassable creek.

Normally, Caleb would have easily outdistanced Latham even with his limp, both youth and familiarity with the area being in his favor. On this day, however, the injury and the storm gave the man the advantage since he could push his way through or over obstacles that Caleb had to go around. The only thing that kept him from getting within shooting distance was an occasional fall, revealed to the boy by a crashing sound followed by a short burst of cursing.

Caleb almost made a fatal mistake, turning to look for Latham and nearly running headlong into the swollen river. He turned his head just in time to spot the danger and stopped at the edge of the crumbling bank, a quick leap backward preventing a tumble into the rushing water as the bank gave way. As he watched, a tree across the expanse of muddy water gave way and fell into the torrent, the current having washed away the dirt holding its roots in place.

He turned north, running along the course of the river, but trying to stay far enough away to avoid falling in. Every now and then he'd have to run close to the bank to avoid a briar patch or a fallen tree, but he was careful to watch his footing.

Unfortunately, Caleb forgot there were more dangers in the river bottoms than just falling in or being caught by Latham. One of these revealed itself with a metallic 'snick' as the carefully concealed otter trap Louis Cook had warned him about sprang shut on Caleb's leg just above the ankle, tumbling him to the ground in excruciating pain. In another hour the creek bank would have eroded the extra few feet and washed away the trap and the danger, but fate and bad timing combined to place his foot in the wrong place at the wrong time.

He frantically yanked at the trap, trying to press the double set springs down to release his leg but he didn't have the strength or the leverage to free himself and every motion of the trap sent waves of nausea crashing through him as the trap grated against the broken bone.

"Well, well, well," a voice said, causing terror to momentarily overwhelm the pain. "Looks like the little rat is in a trap."

Latham walked to the chain holding the trap to the stake driven deep in the ground and yanked it, bringing a scream of pain from Caleb and a grunt of satisfaction from the man.

"I'd rather it was your daddy or that nigger, but I guess you'll have to do."

He stepped back and sat the whiskey jug down, then cradled the rifle a little closer.

"Please Mr. Latham, I didn't do nothing."

"Maybe so, maybe no, but your daddy and that nigger family has made my life hell. The only thing I'm concerned about is they may never find your body.

That's all right though, I'll send the great and powerful Mr. Gandy a letter letting him know what happened to his little boy."

Latham raised the rifle, pulling the hammer back and sighting in on Caleb, who could only lay there waiting for the shot.

It didn't come.

From the bushes to the right, 80 pounds of mad dog hurled himself at Ed Latham, knocking the man backward, the rifle flying from his hands. Bo's snarling was interrupted only by the sound of Latham's screams as the dog laid open his arm, blood streaming and being washed away by the now driving rain. Ed grabbed Bo by the neck, but the loose skin stretched enough to allow the dog a good bite at his face, Ed screaming again as his cheek was ripped to the bone. The dog was unsuccessful in his attempts to reach the man's throat and Ed rolled to the side, throwing the dog off and a few feet away.

As Bo gathered himself for another leap Caleb saw a glint in Latham's hand and screamed, "No Bo!"

Too late.

Just as the dog leapt the pistol in Ed's hand exploded. Bo yelped as the bullet struck him, the impact knocking him into the bushes.

"Goddamned dog," he said, pulling himself to his feet and then kicking the limp body.

Latham glanced at Caleb to be sure he was still trapped, then pulled a handkerchief from his pocket, mopping the blood and rain from his face before wrapping the cloth around his bleeding forearm.

He reached down and picked up the rifle, cursing again as he saw the mud clogging the barrel. Carefully he lowered the hammer and picked up a stick, digging the mud out of the barrel, muttering under his breath. After a minute he gave up, sat the rifle on the ground and turned his attention back to Caleb.

"Where were we?" he asked with a grin, then raised his pistol and pointed it at Caleb.

144

Once again he was interrupted by an explosion of activity as Johnny Robinson ran full into his legs, wrapping his arms around them, the momentum forcing the man backwards.

"Run Caleb, run!" the boy yelled, not realizing Caleb was chained to the spot.

Latham had just managed to regain his balance and raised the pistol to club Johnny when the third surprise, wet blonde hair plastered to her head, erupted from the bushes and added her weight and momentum to Johnny's struggles, pushing Ed back again and causing him to stumble over the rifle and onto the riverbank, which promptly crumbled under him, dumping him and the two children into the swollen waters. Caleb lunged to the side, and his fingers just managed to brush Johnny's hand and Leesie's dress as they disappeared into the river.

CHAPTER 20

Afterwards

Ed Latham's body was recovered a week later, hung up in the roots of a tree where Kisatchie Creek joined with others and eventually flowed into the Red River. His face and body were horribly disfigured as a result of being struck uncountable times by the trees washing downriver. Miss Callie's watch was still in his pocket.

Neither Johnny nor Leesie's bodies were ever found.

Caleb later learned that Bo had been visiting Johnny while Caleb was looking for him. Johnny had brought him home but Bo had pulled loose from the hunk of rope Johnny was using as a leash and taken off at a run, the boy close behind. Leesie had spotted them and the three had retraced Caleb's steps, arriving in time to save him but at a huge cost.

Bo recovered from his gunshot wound although, like his boy, he would always limp. He never became a championship 'coon dog, but several of his descendants did. Bo lived to the ripe old age of 18, passing away in front of the fireplace at Caleb's house, surrounded by a loving family and a fresh litter of blue tick puppies crawling all over him.

Luther and Dora Robinson moved off, their hearts broken at the loss of their beloved Johnny. Caleb heard they had another son a few years later, and he hoped that was true.

Faye Osborne never recovered from Leesie's death. She passed away six months later, dead of a heart attack while working at a laundry in Natchitoches.

Caleb thought it was probably a broken heart that actually killed her.

The flood washed away the turpentine camp, leaving nothing to commemorate the good and bad times and the good and bad people who had lived and died there. Occasionally a hunter will pass over the old grounds, kick at what looks like a rock in the creek and be rewarded by the rich smell of pine which still emanates from the resin piles, now solidified.

Mr. Gandy was offered a job at the company headquarters and Caleb became a city boy. He graduated from high school, went to the Louisiana Normal College, and eventually graduated from Louisiana State University's law school.

During the 60s, Caleb Gandy's name was renowned as a fearless fighter for the civil rights of African Americans. He never told anyone why he was so ferocious on the subject. Likewise, his private endowment of one million dollars to fund the Eloise Osborne scholarship fund provided hundreds of scholarships over the years to lower income students who wanted to become teachers, but they never knew who Eloise Osborne was or who had provided them the scholarship.

****

Thomas Gandy found his father sitting propped against a fence, not far from where he had left his car parked on the side of the road. A historical marker just down the highway told the tale of the turpentine camps and their place in Louisiana history.

He knew from the stories his dad had told him that some of his happiest memories had been at the camp just a few hundred yards into the woods from where his body now sat. On the one occasion he had brought his son here they'd walked the woods in silence, Tommy content just to be with him as Caleb Gandy relived the playgrounds of his youth.

Tommy now stood over his father, looking at him for one of the last times, the leather collar and red bottle clasped in his hands as out of place as the slight smile now etched permanently on Caleb's face. For a moment, only a moment, he thought he heard the sound of a dog joyously barking, as if greeting a long lost master now returning home. Mixed with the sounds of the barks Tommy could swear he heard the laughter of children, and imagined the three friends happily joining hands and running off through the woods to some grand adventure, the dog leaping around them.

Then the moment was gone and the sound faded.

****

Caleb was buried with the leather collar and the red bottle tucked carefully away with him.

THE END

About the Author

Robert D. Bennett was born in Louisiana and spent his childhood there and in Texas.

His Diverse work history has taken him across the United States, Mexico and the Caribbean as well as England, and his books are shaped by the people he has known and the places he has visited.

"If I write about a place, it's because I've visited there and either the place or the people left an impression." Bennett said when asked about the inspirations for his books.

He currently resides in Texas with his wife Karren and his Jack Russell Terrier "Sup" and occasionally his twin sons as they return from College on breaks and his daughter and her husband when they visit.

Coming Soon
Look for more titles by this author
including the Junebug and Noah Chance Series.
Find them at www.RobertDBennett.com
or follow him on
Twitter at RobertTheWriter

Made in the USA
Charleston, SC
03 May 2013